'A bit like Robert E. Ho
with a dash of Fritz Leib

queerness, coping with disability, and found family arise organically within the stories, signalling not a deconstruction of sword & sorcery, but a broader inclusivity.'
Ngo Vinh-Hoi, co-host of the *Appendix N Book Club* podcast

'Intimate, literate and touching scenes erupt into visceral violence; I was reminded of Poe's Hop-Frog.'
Ricardo Pinto, author of *The Stone Dance of the Chameleon*

'Call it New Wave Sword & Sorcery... a reaction to the musclebound masculinity, the unbridled machismo that is found and often-times put at the forefront of Sword & Sorcery. It's good stuff if you're open to the idea of new takes on Sword & Sorcery.'
Rogues in the House podcast

The Red Man
and Others

Angeline B. Adams
&
Remco van Straten

TURNIP
LANTERNS

First digital edition July 2019
First print edition April 2021

ISBN: 978-1-80049-574-6

For more information, contact: angeline.adams@gmail.com
https://linktr.ee/turniplanterns

To our mothers, Celia and Martha

Contents

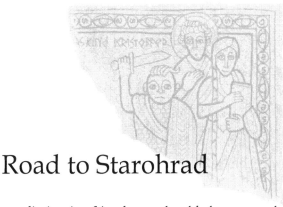

Road to Starohrad

'Of course, my diminutive friend, one should always travel with a heavy pack but a light purse. That's the best way to prevent unpleasantness with roadside ill-wishers.'

'That doesn't make any sense,' Kaila smiled. 'They'd be as likely to strip you of any goods you have as of coin.'

'Hm. Well, you'd know more about this sort of thing.' Master Osgot scraped his throat and clacked his tongue at the horses that pulled the covered wagon, then tried again. 'Of course, one should always travel with a full belly but an empty purse if one wants to outwit the footpad.'

'Slightly better, and at least something you've put into practice. A lot. Has it worked it for you?' She patted her belly and looked up at Master Osgot, in whose shadow she sat. While she was used to everyone being much taller than her, most men seemed small compared to him.

'Oh, tush! You mock my heavy bones, but hark me well, young one; you too will reach that age at which future dreams turn into missed opportunities, and your skin too will lose its tautness, allowing the flesh underneath to expand.'

'Not me,' Kaila said, all trace of levity gone from her voice. 'The day I know I'm in decline is the day I'll die.'

'Decline and death; how certain the young are, and how wary,' Osgot sighed. 'Life doesn't stop at twenty, young maiden, or even at thirty – far away and horrible as that future sounds. Each age comes with its trade-offs, but believe you me, you'll not come out the worse until -' he let his face drop back into the folds of his chins, stretched his lips over his teeth and made his voice a cackle, '- you're a doddery, toothless hag.'

Kaila guffawed. 'You stick to acting, that's where your talent lies! Meanwhile, I won't let any robber get near enough to find out the weight of your purse. A sharp sword and a willingness to use it, those are the best way to deal with them.' Osgot knew this, of course, and that was why he'd hired her.

Osgot wiped the sweat from his forehead, leaving the sculpted curls of his wig slightly askew. He carefully folded his handkerchief and tucked it in the breast pocket of his tunic, leaned his head backwards and closed his eyes, letting the horses follow the road hoof by hoof for themselves. They drove in silence for a while. They'd just passed a crossroads complete with gibbet (occupant deceased), and a sign that they were one day's travel removed from Starohrad. The other roads weren't signposted – in this part of the world all roads led there. The sun beat down mercilessly on their small caravan. The wagons were brightly painted, as was fitting for a troupe of actors, but far muddier and dustier than they had been when Kaila joined them a week earlier. She'd been about to leave the garrison town of Castelwicz on foot when she was drawn by the open-air play put on by Master Osgot to pay for restocking the caravan. When she heard they were going to Starohrad she offered her services. He had looked at her, measured her up and had laughed. Then he'd apologised.

'I thought you wanted to join our little troupe. The stage will harbour all manner of rejects of polite and impolite society. However, were I to allow a woman on the stage, it'd get me excommunicated, hanged, and, worst of all, it would get my player's licence revoked. However, you want to lend us your sword arm in trade for passage to Starohrad? Welcome aboard!'

In the week that followed, Kaila had learned that though his hair might be fake, there was nothing false about the man's character, and if his personality was as big as the body that housed it, then was it matched by his generosity.

Kaila herself had stripped down to her underclothes. Her sword she kept beside her, and nobody who saw the breadth of her shoulders and the corded muscles of her arms and legs would doubt that she knew how to use it.

'There, ahead. Be sharp,' Kaila warned. Further up the road, a group of people were coming towards them. Kaila leaned from the wagon's bench and waved to the other wagons to slow down.

'It's Wheelies,' Osgot said, 'the Brotherhood of the Wheel. Followers of the Wheeled Child. Krzystof. You must have heard of them, surely. No?'

'No. But with those shaved heads and those robes – I know the type. Why are they pushing a giant wheel?'

'As I said: Wheelies. They can be a nuisance, but one

should not hold that against them; our engagement in Starohrad, that will fill both purse and paunch, is through them. The High Priestess Lisanna -'

'She's one of – them?' Kaila nodded to the road in front of them. The white-robed men had stopped their advance and had positioned the massive wooden wheel to block the road. Master Osgot held out his long arm, gesturing the wagons behind them to halt, and reined in his own horses. He turned back to Kaila.

'Oh, indeed she is! She *loves* Krzystof the Uncomplaining Child. Well, actually,' he bent closer, 'young, blond and innocent. That's what she likes. But far be it from me to pass judgment on anyone's peccadilloes. As a whole, the Wheelies are quite harmless, I assure you.'

'She sounds like a right charmer, this Lisanna,' Kaila said. She reached behind her and retrieved her boots. 'Here, out on the road, you can never assume people's intentions. To be too trusting is to get hurt. For all I know this could be a ruse.'

'Such lives of shadow and peril you people of the sword lead. It's no place for a poor actor like myself, for whom mummery and trickery are tools of stagecraft.'

Kaila stood up, slung on her metal-studded, black leather surcoat and buckled on her sword belt.

'Don't you need that?' Osgot asked, pointing at the chain mail vest that still lay behind her in the cart. Kaila shrugged.

'It'd slow me down too much. Well, let's see whether they be chickens or foxes.' She jumped off the wagon and walked towards them. They eyed her up and down as she stood at a twenty-pace distance. She heard snorting laughter and whispers. Indeed, she was small, not even chest high to the shortest of them. Yes, she was a girl. And no, the sword she carried was, naturally, not a very large one.

'Right. Are you going to remove that wheel and make way, or are we going to have a disagreement?' Well, at least they stopped laughing. 'Who's in charge of your lot?'

Out of the dozen or so, one stepped forward. She'd thought it'd be him, the one with the grey, dead eyes; he wasn't one of the men who'd been pushing the wheel forward, nor one of the half dozen whose heads sat low between their shoulders and whose muscular arms stood out from their bodies, gripping their wheel-topped staffs like spears. Neither those who had shuffled behind the wheel, nor their strong-arm companions. Definitely not the one with that beard.

'We ask for a small donation for the Festival of the Wheel.' More a command than a request. He nodded to his side, and a handful of the more heavyset men stepped forward.

'Not interested. Tell your trolls to stand down and make way.' She slid her sword halfway out of its sheath.

'Kaila, really! There is no need for hot-headedness!' She glanced behind her. Master Osgot trotted towards them. His troupe stayed with the wagons; good. Slightly out of breath, Osgot unfurled a roll of paper and stretched to hand it the band's leader. 'I've been commissioned by the High Priestess to stage a play in a month's time, at the conclusion of the Child's festival. It is to celebrate the marriage of the High Priestess Lisanna herself to the Duke of Grindolf. That's the signature of her chief cleric. This would be enough of a contribution, no?'

'Our commission comes from the Child himself, however. Two hundred Kronar would be generous enough, fat man. That, or provide some sport for my men.' Deadeye snatched the paper from the actor's hand and dropped it, grinding it into the ground with his sandal. His men laughed. Kaila saw dull metal in clenched fists.

'Stand back,' she hissed at her employer, and shoved him away. She slid into a crouch and swung her sword. One man dropped screaming with his calf muscles severed, as she hauled in her sword, slicing through another's side, then swung it over her head and let it bite his neck. He dropped like a sack of flour, dead before he hit the ground. She stabbed between a third man's ribs, his raised staff a poor defence, and planted her foot against his chest while she pulled her sword free, sending him and two others sprawling. Two came at her with their staffs, but they hampered each other. It was a short fight in which only one landed a glancing blow before Kaila's sword bit deep twice. She jerked her sword free, ramming her elbow in the guts of the man who'd sidled behind her. She rotated on the balls of her feet, her sword on his throat, while her other hand grabbed and twisted those parts of him that nature did not intend to be grabbed or twisted. He went down on his knees. 'Run or die,' she growled. He ran.

A warning from Osgot came too late to evade the cudgel to her head. She moved with the blow, hit the ground and rolled away. Darkness swam over her vision. She kicked out with both legs to the dark blur that closed in on her and felt bone give beneath her boots. She braced her sword, upwards. A high-pitched scream, then he lay limp on top of her. She pushed him away, rising in a crouch. She kept one hand on the ground to stop herself keeling over, and pointed her sword at the dark circle of the wheel. The murky veil before her eyes dissolved, though not the iron fist that held her head. She glanced round, blinking, each movement of her eyes a jab of pain. A few of the men were running, some were on the ground, screaming. Others were dead.

She rose, her eyes seeking their leader among the few who remained. His comrades moved away from him. He raised his hands and dropped the knife he'd been holding. He slowly walked towards her, until stopped by the tip of her sword against his stomach.

'I underestimated you. I expect many have done, to their cost. Know that there is a place with us for such as you, sister, and you'll -'

Kaila didn't hear his offer. She pushed forwards with her full weight and her sword disappeared in Dead-eye's gut.

'Not. Interested. I told you.' Her face close to his. Tears sprang in his eyes and he nodded slowly. Then she shoved him backwards, dragging her sword up and out as he fell.

'Anyone else?' she challenged the four who were left. From behind the wheel they stared at their leader, who was dying a messy death at Kaila's feet.

'No? I thought not. Now, get lost, before I change my mind.'

They left hurriedly, supporting those wounded who could walk, leaving those who could not to Kaila's mercy. Their leader was left where he lay, his bowels between his outstretched legs and his life draining away rapidly. Osgot looked at him with mounting horror and he looked back, his eyes wide awake now and seeming more alive than before. His mouth gasped without breathing, then he was still.

'Your sword is ravenous, little one, and you are quick to sate its hunger. Why kill a man, when he's already placed himself in your hands?' He stooped and picked up the paper which the dead man had stamped on. It was tattered and streaked with gore; he carefully rolled it back up and tucked it away. Kaila knelt at the man's dead body and cleaned her sword on his white robes.

'When a viper hisses at you, you lop off its head. If you just step over it, it'll nip at your heels.'

'It might, or it might shed its scaly skin and reveal the butterfly inside. That man there will never be able to atone for whatever his misdeeds were.'

Kaila shrugged and rose, sliding her sword into its sheath.

'Samael, Harld, Gaven,' she turned to some of Master Osgot's men, who had hesitantly come closer and indicated the bodies, 'can you clear the road of these so we can be on our way? And can someone get me a cup of strong wine? I've got a banging headache to drown out.' She leaned against the side of the wheel which, miraculously, was still balanced on its broad, iron-clad rim, and massaged her head.

'Excuse me,' a thin voice croaked from beside and below her, 'Would you release a wretch from an awkward position, please?'

A flushed face with blonde curls hung, upside-down, from a lanky body. His name was Sebastien, and the monks had tied him across the wheel some hours earlier.

'I was thirsty and footsore, and fed up with being prodded in the back with their sticks. So, I sat down, and said they'd have to tie me to the wheel to get me moving.'

'Which they did.' Osgot clasped his hands before his face. 'You poor, poor boy. Such suffering heaped upon one so young and innocent!'

'Like the bleeding Child himself,' Kaila said. The questions, she thought, could wait until her head had stopped thumping.

They untied him and cleaned him up a bit while the others cleared the road. The wagons were moved to where, as Master Osgot put it, 'death might hang less thickly,' and there they made camp. Once they'd got a fire going and passed bread and dripping around, Kaila finally got that cup of strong wine, shared with Sebastien and Osgot. One by one the others joined them, though sitting at some distance, and without the songs and merriment that were usual for the players' camp.

'I sat in the Cock and Swine, as usual after a night's work,' Sebastien began. 'People usually leave you alone – it's all long knives and short tempers in there, so if you drink there, people assume you're tougher than you look. The two men that approached me were either very brave, I thought, or foolish. Wheelies. I recognised them by the little cloth wheel they wore on their jerkins.'

'What's all that about, anyway?' Kaila asked. 'Big wheels rolled around, wheels on sticks, now little wheels made of cloth.'

'They had me strapped to the wheel, right?'

'Yeah?'

'Same with Krzystof. Though after wheeling him a-round, they burnt him. But he did not complain! Hence, the Uncomplaining Child.'

'They were going to commit you to the flames?' Osgot grabbed the boy's hands.

'Oh no, they had something worse in mind. But we'll get to that. So, these two are looking around the pub, and they catch me watching them. They nudge each other and sidle over, put on big smiles. One looks a bit of an oaf, the other's slight and I suppose you'd call him good looking. He goes, 'If it would suit the young master, I would to tell him of Krzystof, the Uncomplaining Child.' Both doing their best to look pious. 'Why, it would be a waste of such a fine summer afternoon if I did not personally show you his chapel. It has only today been dedicated, and it's not far from here."

'Recruiters,' Kaila said. Osgot raised an eyebrow, so she explained: 'They'd get paid for anyone they bring in to be baptised. Lots of religions have them.'

'That's what I thought,' Sebastien said. 'It had been a lean day for me, so I thought, why not, and proposed to go willingly for a cut, and save them the trouble of forcing me or getting me drunk first. They were fine with the plan and I followed them.'

10

Kaila shrugged. She'd done worse for money, but she could never bow to any god.

'And indeed, they were recruiters. A simple paid baptism wasn't waiting for me, though. The High Priestess had sent word that she was on the look-out for boys for her harem, so there I went, on my way to Starohrad for that woman's personal fleshpots.'

Osgot's jowls quivered. 'Monstrous! A woman's appetites should never be larger than her instep, lest she stub the toe of decency.'

'Nonsense!' Kaila scoffed. 'A woman has as much right as a man to take what she wants. Men can be pigs, and so can women. Sebastien, what do you do for a living? I doubt you're a simple baker's boy.'

The boy spread his fingers. 'Children are set on their life's path. They get a friendly push or a hard kick, and that's the direction They take. They don't get to choose their own course.'

Kaila shrugged – *Hells, I did*. She didn't quite believe the tale of woe Sebastien sketched, though saw that Osgot lapped it up. One of the men started strumming his lyre, and another blew doleful tones from his flute.

Sebastien's father, a merchant, had died suddenly, leaving large debts and Sebastien an orphan. He was indentured to a weaver, but ran off when the man took to drink and started beating him.

'Since then, with no credentials and no one to speak up for me, I've been forced to live in the shadows. A bit of thieving and a bit of hustling for money. Nothing that would actually hurt anyone, though.'

'Of course. The weaver; did you kill him?' Kaila asked.

'I may have.' Sebastien looked at Osgot's sorrowful face. 'Hurt him. A little bit. In self-defence.'

'I see. And yet, according to Master Osgot here, if a girl were to do the same in your position, she should be condemned for it.'

She crossed her arms and leaned back. Lyre and flute fell silent. Master Osgot raised his hands, warding off her gaze.

'Once again I concede. Just as all men cannot afford to be gentlemen, not all girls can be ladies. Not that you are not a lady, in your own particular fashion. However, to become an animal is a whole other matter, and I cannot indulge one who would subject such as Sebastien to her vile lusts. I have decided: we shall turn our wagons round and we shall not play for her.'

All stared at him.

'Great,' muttered one of his men. Harld just sighed and threw down his plate, while Samael started complaining about the pay they'd miss out on, with the rest nodding and aye-ing. Kaila remained silent, biting her lower lip. She went to Osgot and whispered in his ear. Very quickly, he rose and gestured for silence.

'Roll up your tongues! You want to play and earn your pay, yes? Then we will direct our wagons to Starohrad, and we will give the High Priestess a performance she will long remember!'

Of course they agreed, even if they wondered about their leader's sudden change of heart. With dusk drawing a veil over the horrors of the day, a better mood descended on the camp. Songs were sung and parts rehearsed while cups were filled and wine skins emptied. Master Osgot covered Sebastien with a blanket, chuckling about the boy's ability to sleep through the company's laughter and loud singing. He heard out Kaila's plan, once she had been able to think it through some more.

'With such a mind as yours, it's a pity you've chosen the way of the sword. You could accomplish so much,' he told her.

'Who says I won't?' She winked and disappeared into the night. She only returned when everyone had retired, and even when she'd lain down on her own pallet, she lay awake for a long time.

*

Not long after dawn they had the wagons moving towards Starohrad again. A nervous energy had taken hold of the company; they felt something new approaching and were eager to meet it. Kaila and Sebastien each kept apart from the others. Kaila walked ahead of the caravan, nursing her own thoughts and a hangover, while Sebastien sat in Osgot's wagon, preparing for what would be his part in the play Kaila had devised.

'Would you mind doing some hustling and thieving, if it means getting one over on the High Priestess and the Wheelies?' she'd asked him.

'Tell me what to do,' he'd replied. Privately, he wondered whether he ought to stay out of it, slip back to his life in the shadows. But there was no future there.

Nothing worth having grows in the shadows, only weeds.

Master Osgot stuck his head through the canvas flaps. It was time.

While the company settled in, their wagons parked in a small courtyard in the city, Kaila, Sebastien and Osgot set off towards the bridge that connected the City with the Citadel. Osgot wore his gaudiest tunic and a hat that was really too large for him. Kaila had donned her full battle gear and Sebastien was clothed in rags and had his hands bound in front of him.

The Citadel loomed over the Bottoms, its marble-clad buildings throwing the descendants of its builders into shadow for much of the day. After crossing the Wist, the bridge became a causeway that was elevated over the patched roofs of the Bottoms, where human waste littered the streets and cheaply built tenements were piled up so close together that they prevented each other from collapsing. No need for the wealthy burghers of Starohrad to dirty their boots.

'The gentle breeze carries a mean smell from the river,' Osgot said, wrinkling his nose. It wasn't only the river either; he pointed out litter and filth where the sandstone villas and cobbled streets had previously been pristine. It wasn't busy, not at all as busy as it should be, he noted. He'd been in Starohrad years earlier, when he was younger and less brilliant than he'd thought. Back then the Causeway, with its famous Boulevard of Kings, had been a place where people went for a leisurely stroll, to see and be seen. Now the only people they saw appeared to be in a hurry, either coming from the Citadel or hurrying towards it. And nobody looked at each other, except for the odd furtive glance.

'They pulled them all down, the old kings.'

The sight of the empty plinths on the bridge held Osgot back. The largest recognisable piece of rubble that lined the parapets was part of a hand, fingers still outstretched in a gesture of blessing.

'Good old Mirek. They got you too, then.' He shook his head and sniffed. Kaila looked at him, but he kept his face turned away from them.

'We must move on,' Kaila said. 'We're being watched.' She'd spotted the followers of Krzystof from the moment they stepped onto the Causeway. Their dress was sombre, adorned only with the four-spoked wheel. She wondered what they'd wear if the Child had died of starvation. A little later they found their way barred by an entire procession of them: about six dozen men, women and children, chanting as they shuffled along.

Bless the Uncomplaining Child,
Pray the Child to save us.

'Krzystof 's Prayer, it's called,' Osgot explained. 'You shall enjoy it on many occasions in - Hullo!' He was rudely shoved aside by one of the cassocked men. Kaila's hand flew to her sword, but Osgot held back her arm.

'Leave it be. There's a time and place for that, but it's not here and now. We mustn't give those roaming eyes anything to land on. Here, we're above the guardhouse, Kaila. We'd best part ways.'

'If you say so, boss. You know what to do?'

'Child! Really! I'm an artist! I had at my feet the – never mind that now.'

Kaila winked at them and disappeared into the crowd which had gathered to watch the Wheelies. Osgot jerked the rope on which he led Sebastien.

'Down these stone steps we tread, young man, whether they lead to infamy or oblivion.'

The guardhouse was built into one of the pillars that held up the Causeway arches. Aside from the practicalities, it had been built as a beacon of civilisation and order, but its windows had long been bricked up, its stone decorations hacked away and its walls defaced.

Osgot brought the attending guard out of his station with a loud knock on the heavily studded door. He finally appeared, a grizzled veteran. His uniform was incomplete, and a small metal wheel gleamed incongruously on his breast. He yawned and was clearly annoyed by this breach of his routine. Osgot laid it on thick to break through the man's apathy.

'This young man tried to rob me at knife point. If my brave travelling companions hadn't stepped in, I don't know what might have happened!'

The guard stared at them. Without a word he turned around and had almost closed the door behind him when Osgot hastily added, 'And he made insults to Krzystof to boot!'

The man was back out, sighing. 'Now, that's a different matter. Those words, once heard, need listened to. Is that true, young man?'

Sebastien dutifully nodded.

'Well, my lad, it's the chopping block or the habit, then. What'll you have?'

'I'll take the habit.' Sebastien raised his bound wrists. 'Need both my hands, don't I?'

The guard scribbled down statements from them both. Osgot signed it with a flourish while Sebastien scratched an X on the page.

'You be a model novice and make something of yourself,' Osgot urged, as the guard closed the iron barred door behind the boy.

'I'll check on the boy's progress,' he said, ensuring that the guard would do his duty. The old soldier walked him outside and nodded upwards.

'Do you ever wonder whether the High Priestess is looking out of her window and watching us?' he asked. 'Does she care about us doing double shifts down here, while she's got most of the guards waiting on her up there?' He sighed and sat down on the little bench next to the door.

'Nah, she's got no time for old codgers like me. She's too busy with those boys she surrounds herself with. They remind her of the Child, and their innocence inspires her.'

'I've heard tell she chooses them for their looks,' Osgot said. The guard shot him a warning glance. 'Though I wouldn't say anything like that myself, of course.'

Osgot put a slipper on the stone steps back to the Causeway, then turned around again. 'The statues of the Kings, don't you miss them?'

'Sometimes. But apparently, they led people to the

worship of false idols, and so they had to go. Praise Krzystof, good sir.' He drew a quick circle in the air.

'Praise Krzystof,' Osgot mumbled.

*

A choking heat clung to the Citadel's inner walls. The leaves of the olive trees had turned brittle and brown, the arches and fluted columns of the courtyard's galleries shimmered, and the fountain nymphs touched mere dust with their stone feet. Workmen cursed, casting furtive glances over their shoulders as they rested a moment, then slung another wooden beam or another bundle of floorboards on their hardened backs. For the past few days, all the bits and pieces that made a stage had been unloaded from the ox carts and directed to their proper place by the castle's master carpenter. He'd compared the marks on each slat, beam and panel with those on the drawing on the table in front of him and ensured that all joints were fastened tightly, instructing his crew where to wrap a weak joint with rope, make emergency repairs and replace any missing pieces.

By mid-afternoon the basic structure of the two-storey stage was mounted against the Citadel's outer wall and Osgot inspected it with the master carpenter.

'You have built an excellent stage, Master Halbrecht. It will be a pleasure to play on. I wager you'll be eager to see the fruits of your labours?'

'The art for me is in getting the thing up without fuss and bother. Don't mind me, Master Osgot, but mummers prancing about and spouting poetry are not for me. I'd rather spend the evening with a good mug of ale and a pretty girl.'

The hand that he raised to his mouth in a drinking motion was hardened with calluses, Osgot saw, and the arm he had around his imaginary woman was sinewy and sunburnt.

Most of the workmen were sent home. Osgot instructed the few that remained to put in place the curtains, large props and background canvasses. He smiled as the wooden structure slowly turned into the make-believe world his people would inhabit that evening. Many of the Citadel's servants found things to do in the vicinity of the stage, and Osgot indulged their curiosity.

'Does a holy man live in the grotto?' they ask him, and 'How do you reach the balcony?'

'Perhaps,' he answered, as a marsh of green and grey sail cloth was draped in front of the cave. 'Stage magic,' he said, and winked as the balcony was enriched with paper garlands and bright cloth flowers. If they'd been there earlier, they'd have seen the ladders on each side of the painted forest, now hidden from view by the grotto and the labourer's cottage.

'What will the play be about?' a maid asked, beaming her excitement. 'Will there be a handsome prince in it?'

'You'll have to wait to find out what it's about, but I can promise you that there will certainly be the handsomest of princes.' None of the servants were invited to the play, but he knew that whoever could be missed from their duties, even for a moment, would hang out of the palace's windows. Sometimes he felt that the servants of a place were his true audience.

'Excuse me, are you Master Osgot?' The voice that had joined him on the stage, though not an adult one, had none of the humility of the serving staff. He turned, straightening his back. The boy was dressed in an immaculate white habit, and wore a simple wooden Wheel around his neck. Sebastien.

'Yes, that's me,' Osgot introduced himself, and gave the boy a quick bow from the waist, 'manager, playwright and lead actor of this fine troupe.' Though Osgot towered over the boy, he felt himself shrinking under his cold glare. Sebastien certainly played his part well: a natural for the stage. He sighed.

'Is anything wrong, Master Osgot?'

'Never mind me; the silliness of an old actor. I was ruminating on the fleetingness of the stage; we work for weeks toward a single performance. The next day, the costumes are put away, the stage is broken down, and nothing remains but the memories.'

Sebastien scraped his throat and nodded to the small platform opposite the stage. 'Is that for us?'

'Yes, that's where the High Priestess, the Duke and you boys will sit. The benches at the sides are for the other spectators.' He saw that the boy was judging the distance between the stage and the platform. 'A bit of distance is ideal, so they don't have to crane their necks, and the view of the upper stage is unobstructed.' Also, this distance had been dictated by protocol, like the dozen guards who were to be stationed just in front of the platform. This had been discussed in detail with the Captain of the Guard weeks ago, even before it was agreed which of the plays in the company's repertoire would be performed.

Sebastien turned towards the stage. 'Are you all set for the evening?'

'Yes, we're well prepared; every one of us knows his part.'

'Well done. Well done. And you were saying about balcony...?'

'Yes, the balcony, it's where the play begins. It starts with a princess; you'll like her.' He looked sideways at Sebastien and wondered just how much of a favourite he was with the Priestess, and whether he had used his position to satisfy his curiosity. No, he decided, that'd be too risky. More likely he'd been sent by her, and she'd be expecting a full report later. The boy walked around the painted forest and pointed to one side.

'Up here?' he asked, already climbing the ladder. He certainly was fast. Osgot scrambled up in his wake, and found him leaning over the balcony.

'Careful!' he urged. Sebastien just ambled across the balcony patting the stage's back cloth, on which a palace interior had been sketched in bold colours and outlines. He gave a coiled up rope a shove with his sandal.

'What's this for?'

Osgot explained how the villain would clamber down from the balcony, and demonstrated the breakaway piece of its railing.

'That's ingenious!' the boy said, apparently not considering that he could've lain below with his neck broken, had the railing not been bolted tightly in place prior to the performance. Osgot masked his relief when Sebastien bade him goodbye and disappeared back into the palace.

*

From their high windows, servants and off-duty guards cheered the tumblers and jugglers who careered about the stage as the courtyard-side benches slowly filled with well-groomed men and their ladies. The platform opposite the stage remained empty to the last. Osgot stood hidden behind the stage and glanced at the palace's main entrance. Finally, the richly carved doors opened. He signalled the musicians on stage. Effortlessly their rollicking tune changed into a solemn beat. The acrobats departed, the babble of voices hushed, and necks both in the courtyard and above craned towards the palace's open maw.

First, the naked little girls appeared. They were covered in silver leaf that made them shimmer in the sunlight. They carried baskets full of dried flower petals, which they tossed into the air. Two smiling matrons in white capes carried thin reeds, applied as whips to spur on any girl whose skipping and flower-tossing seemed less enthusiastic. Then came the High Priestess Lisanna and the Duke of Grindolf, followed by two bejewelled thrones carried by a dozen little boys. The boys, too, were nude and covered in silver leaf.

Lisanna was dressed in many layers of white, but the delicate fabric was folded and cut in such a manner that they accentuated her figure, rather than hiding it. Her red hair was worn without a veil, piled high on her head and held in place with silver clasps and pins. Copper dust gave her head the appearance of a sun radiating from beneath her halo of hair. Around her neck she wore a heavy gold chain, on which the sigil of her office hung: the solid gold disc of the Wheel, engraved with the image of a young man, its rim inlaid with precious stones. Beside her spectacle, people hardly looked at the Duke.

They were followed by a dozen older boys in white robes, the Child's Children. On the musician's beat they chanted Krzystof's Prayer with crystal voices. They were led by Sebastien. Among the other Children he appeared almost defiantly ordinary, but Osgot understood why Lisanna favoured him. His boyish looks held a promise of the man he'd be, and he carried himself with both piety and pride, innocence and fire.

The guests of honour installed themselves in their satin-covered thrones. Osgot gave a signal to the musicians, walked out and bowed. He held out his hand to stop the smattering of applause which he pretended was bigger, then spoke.

'I trust you'll approve my words, from first to end,
and that afterwards I may still call you friend.'

With this, he bowed again and left the stage. The play began.

'Sebastien, hand me my wine, will you dear?'

Sebastien, standing at the High Priestess' right side, ducked his head and reached out. A servant standing behind them handed him the goblet. Sebastien took a sip, closed his eyes, and let the spiced liquid wash through his mouth. He swallowed, opened his eyes and nodded gravely at his mistress. She smiled at his bit of pantomime and accepted the goblet. She returned her attention to the stage, her free hand playing through the thick curls of one of the twin boys in front of her.

'What was she saying?' She bent to her left side.

'The princess? She's waiting for her betrothed. He's overdue, apparently.' The Duke studied the character who'd appeared on the balcony. He narrowed his eyes, and his thumb and index finger massaged his chin.

Lisanna elbowed him. 'You do know that the princess is being played by a young man in a wig, don't you?'

'Pretty, though,' the Duke shrugged and continued his observation of the princess, who now leaned over the balcony, scouring the imaginary countryside left and right, shielding her eyes from the imaginary sun's glare with her hand.

'Where then my knight, who'd surely not tarry,' she cried out,
To honour his pledge, to take me in marriage
His bravery true, his nerve undefiled
Though, never so brave as t' Uncomplaining Child!'

A drumbeat from off-stage signified a heavy footfall that disturbed the princess's contemplation.

'Is it him?' she asked. Then she saw the creature that leaped towards her, a ragged cape billowing out behind its squat and hunched shape. The player's face was hidden by a beaked mask rendered in sun-hardened paper-and-glue mush, and a tatterdemalion costume suggested feathers and fur. The creature raised its paws at the princess. Sharp talons were mounted on heavy, leather gloves. She screamed and hid her face in her hands.

'What heinous shape do I espy,
Who dares my royal self to steal?
With such as you I'll only lie,
as the Child lay on the Wheel.'

The princess sighed loudly and dropped to the floor. The monster laughed and picked her up, then heaved her still form over his shoulder.

'He's quite a find, isn't he?' The Duke leaned over to the High Priestess. 'I don't think I've seen him before, for how could you forget someone that grotesque? And strong too!' He watched in fascination as the monster flung a rope over the railing and slid down it, the Princess' body slung over his shoulder.

'It's a trick, of course,' Lisanna said. 'When she fell behind the ivy that covers the balustrade, she was replaced by a dummy.'

'He joined the troupe just a month ago.' Sebastien had moved behind them. He lowered his head between theirs. 'Master Osgot told me he's a mysterious fellow who keeps to himself, and is never seen without his mask. They say he even pretends to be the monster off-stage.'

The Duke shifted in his seat, away from Sebastien. 'Master Osgot may be proud of his players,' he said, his cheeks reddening with indignation, 'but less so of his writing. What torturous lines descend from that stage!'

Lisanna cleared her throat meaningfully. Her chief clerk had had quite a hand in ensuring that the play properly displayed the merits of Krzystof, the Uncomplaining Child. Sebastien resumed his seat, and the three of them dutifully continued watching the play.

The prince, played by Master Osgot himself, swore to find or at least avenge his bride. He fought outlaws and peasants who were under the monster's spell. Finally, a chase round the whole stage ended in the monster's swamp, with the princess tied to a dead tree and the prince's sword at the creature's throat.

'Loathsome thing, neither man nor beast
Of impure blood, in darkness made
You'd warm your skin on her golden light
But instead will find my cold steel blade.'

The prince puffed out his chest and raised his wooden sword, bringing it down on the shaggy head. Instead of falling to its knees, however, the creature took a step forward.

'Not so!' it spat, and planted a foot on Osgot's stomach. With a swift push, Osgot was sent sprawling backwards. The monster walked to the edge of the stage and raised its taloned hand to point at the High Priestess.

'You glut yourself on power, gold and youth,' it said,
Now put aside your wealth and face the truth!'

'I'll forgive you this doggerel, girl,' grunted Osgot, still lying on the boards. 'But get on with it. Don't keep your audience waiting!'

'Your piousness and zeal are hollow,
An empty soul your people follow.'

All eyes were on the High Priestess. She responded to the monster's challenge like the seasoned performer she was. At first, she did not visibly react at all. Then her hands gripped the arm rests of her throne, and very slowly she rose.

'Sacrilege! Guards!' Her scream seemed to come from deep inside her. She whipped her head round, and found herself eye to eye with Sebastien, with the cool blade of his knife against her throat. With his free arm, he held her against his own body, the hand forcing her head up. Her eyes widened and she made a gurgling sound. The Duke yelped and scrambled out of his chair, falling off the dais.

'Drop your swords!' Sebastien yelled. He swung himself and Lisanna round and repeated his command. The sound of steel clattering on the cobbles echoed between the castle walls.

'Sebastien,' Lisanna said, when he released his grip on her throat a little, 'You are a disappointment.'

He didn't answer.

The creature leaped off the stage and, grabbing one of the discarded swords, bounded over to them.

'Off with it!'

The crowd gasped.

Lisanna tried to back away from the stunted figure in the ragged costume, but froze when the knife edge bit in her flesh.

'It's not your head I'm after, lady.' From under the beaked mask, Kaila laughed, still maintaining the deep voice of the monster. She hooked the point of her sword under the heavy links of Lisanna's chain and lifted it over her head. She used the sword so deftly that Sebastien's knife hardly left Lisanna's throat.

'Let's go,' Kaila said to him. He admired her daring and energy; quite a contrast with the languid grace of the woman in whose company he spent most of the past month.

They pushed Lisanna before them to the stage. If the guards had any thought of stopping them, they were hindered by the courtiers who darted about, not wanting to miss anything and trying to use the guards as their personal shields. Master Osgot had left the stage; he and his troupe would be halfway across the causeway bridge by now. Kaila wished she'd had the chance to thank him, but knew he'd be safer in the future if he kept well out of their affairs.

Sebastien pushed Lisanna to the balcony via the stairs behind the scenery. Kaila, sword and Lisanna's chain in one hand, swiftly scaled the seemingly sheer wall of the set on the outside. The ladder she used was carefully disguised with vines and flowers. Excited courtiers pointed at her. Servants pushed and pulled at each other behind the palace windows. To them, her ascent seemed an act of super-human strength.

Kaila climbed on the balustrade and raised Lisanna's chain with its big, golden wheel. She projected her voice:

'If like me of humble birth, have no remorse,
Take what they owe you, and if you must use force.
Destroy the Wheel!'

A whoop sounded from a palace window. Kaila smiled for that brave servant, hidden amongst her fellows. She jumped from the wooden balustrade and aimed her sword at the High Priestess's heart. From under the layers of her costume she retrieved a few feet of rope, which she tossed to Sebastien.

'Good work, kid!' she said.

'Thanks! If I'd had to sing one more dirge about that bloody Child, I'd have screamed. Now, let's write the final act of this play. Hands behind your back, wrists together,' he commanded. Lisanna complied silently, with fury in her eyes. Sebastien wound the rope around her wrists and knotted it securely, then handed the end of the rope to Kaila. Kaila kicked against the breakaway section of the balustrade. Gasps sounded when it clattered loudly on the wooden stage below. Lisanna darted a quick look at the gap, then lunged past Sebastien. Kaila was pulled off balance yet kept hold of the rope. She stumbled, landed on one knee, then found a pillar against which to brace her foot. Without dropping her sword, she grabbed the rope with her other hand too, looping it around her wrist. Lisanna let out a yelp as her arms were pulled taut behind her. Kaila righted herself and with Sebastien she forcefully dragged, then pushed, the struggling woman to the gap in the balcony.

'Stop squirming if you want to live!' she hissed. The other woman curled her toes over the edge of the balcony's floor; only Kaila's pull on her wrists kept her from plummeting. Kaila allowed her to take one step back, and stood next to her, sword pointed at the woman's throat.

'Will anyone fight me for the lady's life?' she shouted. 'How about you there on that throne? Yes, you. Grindolf.' A wave of voices rolled to the dais, where the Duke sat, staring at the monster, the boy and his bride-to-be. With all eyes on him, he slowly rose, beckoning the Captain of the Guards, who shot to his side. A quick word, a nod from the soldier, and orders were barked. The Duke smoothed his tunic, briskly stepped down the dias and strode to the castle's gate, with the full palace guard in his wake.

'No!' the High Priestess screamed.

The palace door opened and closed in silence, then the noise burst from the crowd.

'String her up!' someone shouted, and 'Chuck her!'

'Bring her to my house at midnight when the wife's asleep!' another tried, and more lewd suggestions came, followed by laughter.

'Destroy the Wheel!' Kaila heard from one of the palace windows. She smiled behind her mask.

'Well, you heard them. I guess it's curtains for you.' Kaila stepped backwards and raised her sword.

'No, don't.' Sebastien said. 'Look at her. You've already won.'

Lisanna had fallen to her knees, her shoulders shaking. She looked up at the raised sword, her face a mask of hate, black tracks of kohl running down her cheeks.

'Do it!' she muttered between sobs. 'See how the people like you then!'

'Do you want to be a hero, or do you want to be like her?' Sebastien prompted.

Kaila sighed and put her sword away. 'Here,' she said, tossing him a pair of leather gloves like her own. She hauled up the rope that she had descended with in the play's first act. She confirmed that it was moored securely and tossed it over the side of the citadel's rampart. She looked down. Good. The castle groundsmen had become complacent and had allowed plenty of shrubbery to thrive.

Sebastien went over the wall first. The slide to freedom was the most exhilarating moment of his life so far. Kaila bowed once more to her audience.

'Good luck, sweetheart,' she said to the High Priestess, still in her demon's voice, then vaulted over the wall.

*

They took up lodgings that Kaila had arranged in the Bottoms, right under Lisanna's nose. She'd paid in advance, and enough for their landlady to be discrete, but not so much as to make her greedy.

That first day after their escape from the Citadel, Kaila teased Sebastien mercilessly. She called him 'Lisanna's pet', asking whether he'd not rather go back to his 'mama up there,' and whether the Priestess granted him any special favours.

'Yes,' Sebastien answered, fed up with her taunting. He told her exactly what he'd been made to do for the High Priestess, and what she'd done to him. Kaila stopped laughing, and the subject was not mentioned again.

Sebastien ventured out to dispose of Lisanna's Wheel the day after that.

'One city's alternative economy is much like another's. I'll find a fence,' he'd said, and the jewels indeed were easy enough to get rid of. Once pried off the wheel, they looked pretty generic, as rubies and emeralds went. The wheel itself they had to hack into tiny pieces; it was just too recognisable, and no fence would want to take it off their hands. Intact and complete, the Wheel's value would have been many times higher than he'd got for its component parts, but they knew he'd never have found a buyer for it whole - not without risking their necks into the bargain. Even so, they'd done alright out of it, both of them, even considering the weeks of work it had cost them - him in the white habit, her in the demon's mask.

The blow to the egos of the Duke and the High Priestess demanded that something must not only be done, but seen to be done. Nevertheless, looking for a blond boy and a dwarf in the uncooperative Bottoms was like looking for a needle in a haystack. Various search parties upset the Bottoms, but whenever the knock on the door came, Kaila disappeared out of the window into its alleys and entries, and the soldiers would find a young woman in her sickbed in the dark, with long red hair that was, if anyone had looked closer, made of picked and dyed rope.

The continuing sorties by the city Guard into the Bottoms raised the ire of its various unelected leaders. Their businesses had been disrupted and their hold on the neighbourhood undermined already when the cult of the Child spread its tendrils through the quarter. The gang leaders set aside decades of internal politics and mistrust, and convinced their people that the promises of succour to the poor and hope for the desperate would not come from above; not from the Child. In the ensuing bloody riots of what would be called the Bottoms Rebellion, throat after throat picked up the battle cry, first heard by the Citadel's courtiers, and the servants who had brought it down the steps to their own streets:

'Destroy the Wheel! Destroy the Wheel!'

Staring down from the Citadel ramparts, the Duke thought deeply and sighed. perhaps, he decided, they had a point. Where had all of this begun? With the Wheel coming to Starohrad. What had it got him? Was he loved? Respected? Feared, even? By his people? His betrothed? He sighed again, then sent for his Captain of the Guard.

The next morning, a single emissary of the Duke descended to the Bottoms to announce that the people of Starohrad could consider the Wheel broken, and another went up the stairs to Lisanna's private quarters to announce that she could consider the wedding off. She took only a few hours to pack her belongings and leave town.

To celebrate his new commitment to his people, the Duke announced a Festival to honour the Old Kings. He commissioned Master Osgot, fully cleared of all blame in the unfortunate disgrace of the High Priestess, to orchestrate a pageant.

'There's just one condition,' the said. 'I will permit no dwarfs!'

Osgot brushed off the Duke's concern. 'Our tales will be tall, and our actors will stand taller still in your estimation.'

*

And then one morning, as the whole town made itself ready for the Pageant of the Old Kings, two ponies sauntered along the road leading out of town. Towards noon they came to a crossing. Kaila glanced over her shoulder, but Starohrad had long disappeared from view.

'Well,' she said, 'this is where we say goodbye. That way lies Rhispar. I'm going to see what's happening on the other side of the mountains.'

He nodded. 'I still think we should go into business together,' he said.

'Sebastien, do I look old enough yet to be mothering you?'

'You wound me, Kaila, you really do. And it's a harsh world. Do you not want someone who's got your back?'

'The road I walk, I walk alone. Always have. I'll not have anyone saying I crave or need their protection.' She adjusted her belt, where the weight of her sword hung reassuringly. 'Besides, we're too recognisable together.' She adopted a Northern drawl, such as one heard on the other side of the mountains: 'Y'mean the laddie and t' dwarfen soldier? Yah, they went yonder, so they did!'

He laughed. 'True, true. Well, since you're set on it, let's embrace as friends!' He steered his pony close to hers and leaned into her.

'Okay, kid. That's enough.' She patted his back and then pushed him away.

Sebastien clacked his tongue and nudged his pony in the direction of Rhispar. 'Goodbye, Kaila, until we meet again.'

Kaila watched him for a bit, then took the road to the blackened mountains. It was a glum sort of day, between the rain and, she realised, their parting. She'd grown used to the boy, and it had been a long time since she'd had anything resembling family.

'Come on, Kaila. You ride alone,' she reminded herself. She had her sword on her belt and a small fortune in her purse, which would see her comfortably through the next few months. She patted the purse under her jerkin, but no coin jingled. Her purse was gone.

She turned her pony, but it wasn't necessary to ride Sebastien down. He was already waiting for her at the crossroads. He looked quite pleased with himself. She took her time to catch up with him.

'Alright,' Kaila said. 'you win.'

The Red Man

Ymke held the knife so tightly that her hand hurt.

'Use it if you have to,' Ymke's father had said when he handed her the large carving knife. It was old, but sharp. 'Use it. Don't be a fool; don't just make threats with it.'

Ymke sat in the dark on a wooden chest containing all her belongings. She replaced the cover of the small hole in the outer wall, through which she'd watched until the sun was gone. The sun had sunk through the sky and the birds that nested in the eaves ceased their scratching and settled for the night. Smoke plumes in the distance had marred the summer sunset and shown where opposing armies had made their camps. Between those fires, they'd clashed. Ymke knew that the fighting was long over, and that soldiers roamed the countryside in search of coin, food, or whatever else they hungered for. The rough male voices outside were alarming but not unexpected.

'No, you watch over him, boy!' said one, and others sniggered.

Three men, probably more. They entered the barn, their footsteps on the other side of the partition loud and threatening. The cows mooed at the intrusion.

'Cows! I've got cows at home; I'm sick of looking at

bloody cows. Come on,' said one, and they left, only for her terror to crest again as she heard them burst through the farmhouse door beyond the brick wall she sat against. They called out. Of course, there was no answer. She heard a stomping of boots and a clangour of tin plates, heard chairs being pulled across the flagstones. They talked and laughed; what of, she couldn't make out. She heard more of their stomping about, then the crashing of what must be the sideboard.

'- time for that. You can sleep when you're dead!' said a voice. The doors to the cupboard bed had opened.

'Just want to see what the bastard has hidden in here,' another voice answered, just on the other side of the wooden partition. Slow, drawling. An Easterner. Creaks told her when he climbed into her father's bed and fumbled about turning over the mattress, and a loud thump reverberated through her when his shoulder hit the boards. Ymke stifled a scream, but the catches of the secret panel held.

'Nothing but turnips and the old man's fleas,' the Easterner said, and she heard his boots hit the floor. She slowly released her breath, but kept hold of the knife. Then they left, the front door slamming carelessly in their wake.

She slowly uncovered her spy hole as the men made their way round the house. In the gloaming she saw that there were five of them altogether, ragtag and bloodied. One was in a bad way, and a young lad had been left to watch over him. The lad stared with big eyes and open mouth at the ham gnawed by an older soldier with a stringy beard. They all wore red, to set them apart from the

Westerners, but where the others wore red tunics and sashes, the slack-jawed youth only had a red rag tied across his chest. His boots were mismatched.

Stringy-beard shouted a command. One of the soldiers belched, her father's beer jug smashed against the wall and then they set off, carrying their wounded comrade between them. They would only carry him so far, Ymke knew. If he got any worse, they'd leave him for carrion, and the youth would have matching boots.

The moon was up by the time Ymke heard the wheels of her father's cart, followed by the lowing of the cattle as her father entered the barn. There was a double kick against the partition, followed by silence. She must stay where she was. She tensed, listening to the groans of her father, the thumps and shuffling sounds. He was dragging something heavy.

Two taps then sounded high on the wall, and two more. It was safe to come out. She moved the wooden catches that locked the partition in place, and blinked in the lantern-light. He had the closed-off look that he always wore when he came back from a battlefield forage, but there was also something different, an excitement she hadn't seen in a long time.

'I brought -' he whispered, but then just gestured. 'I need your help. But you mustn't shout.' She nodded and followed him to the barn.

An enormous pair of muddy feet hung over the edge of the cart that her father had backed into the stall. Her first impression of the figure on the cart was immense bulk. Then his skin, furrowed like the fields outside. His shape rippled and wavered with every shallow breath, with every slight movement. She stared, was drawn into the pulsating form, then suddenly felt revulsion.

'A troll!' She lunged back to the safety of her father and made a warding gesture.

'No, Ymke. A man. Though I've never seen one like him before. Not even when -' he checked himself. Ymke caught a quick look of regret, as he closed off the memories of a different life. He hung the lamp on a hook over the stall.

'Kicked in the head by a horse, I think,' her father said, moving the lamp closer to show a face swollen and bruised on one side, and a shaven skull caked with blood and mud.

'Get rags and water and your sewing things,' her father said.

They worked deep into the night, at first together, then in turns as their energies flagged. Her father inspected the giant first, lamp in hand, slowly working his way round. He lifted limbs and pushed flesh, calling out the injuries as he found them, so that Ymke too would remember them. She stopped seeing a troll or even a man of enormous proportions, and saw instead what she'd learned to see in an animal that had fallen ill or was giving birth: a puzzle of skin, flesh and bone that needed solving, with death the cost of failure. She saw that the twisting spirals and curls that had dizzied her eyes were elaborate tattoos and raised welts that covered his whole body. The skin underneath was red; not the red of rust, not red in the face as people are in anger, but true red, and all over his skin. No, not a troll, Ymke thought, but if this was a man then he was one created by unnatural means.

She threaded her needle and started work on the biggest of the giant's wounds, a deep gash between his ribs. His skin was tough, and hardened where it was covered with scars, and she had to be careful not to break her needle. At first hesitant, soon the work progressed swiftly: squeeze, stitch, squeeze, stitch, with an occasional wiping away of blood.

'What was it like?' She bit through the thread and moved on to the next of the giant's many wounds. She'd asked her father before, and only on the bleakest of winter nights would he talk of the stench and the bloated crows, the dogs lapping up blood: 'And we poor devils among them, are we any better?' The following morning, it would be as if he'd never disclosed such doubts, and he'd be brisk when they butchered the cavalry horse, sorted the scraps of metal and cleaned the clothes.

Now her father just looked at her, eyes black pools in the shadows of the lantern. He bent back over the giant.

'His arm's broken and the bone needs to be set,' he said. He told her to sit on the giant and hold his shoulder down with her weight. He pulled the limb and pushed at muscle until he was satisfied. Nausea shot through her as she heard bone scraping over bone.

'Now we need to secure the limb,' he said, wiping the sweat from his brow. She slid off the cart and went to the pile of odds and ends of wood in the corner of the barn, bringing back those she thought would best serve.

She applied a thick layer of honey to draw the bad humours from the broken arm, and handed her father a piece of calfskin. Her father carefully wound it around the arm, and bound the limb tightly between the splints with strips of rag.

Eventually, they'd done all they could for the giant. 'Go and get some sleep,' her father said. 'It's up to the gods now to decide his fate.'

*

The morning sun had already drawn the fog from the fields when Ymke stepped out of her bed. The night had taken its toll on her, and she had to walk carefully so the throbbing ache in her leg would not turn into a stabbing pain. She met her father in the barn. Ymke saw that he had already milked the cows and led them to the field, and that he'd begun bringing in the early hay. He had dark circles under his eyes, and greeted her with a wan smile.

'You did well last night. He may still die, but at least has a chance of living. See what you can do for him.'

She went to the stall and once again she was taken aback by the size of the man. He was still unconscious, though he stirred a little in his slumber.

Now that more light streamed in through the opened barn doors, she could better see how the inked patterns and raised scars on the red skin amplified the musculature and movement of the giant's body. His face, too, was completely covered with lines, giving him the appearance of a permanent snarl and enormous wide-open eyes. She recalled her initial horror of the night before and imagined him on the battlefield, like a grown man in a melee of children. His size and his marked skin would terrify his enemies, and his strength would crush them.

She prepared a thick paste of healing herbs and churned butter, and carefully peeled off the sodden bandages. He didn't react when she washed the remnants of blood and filth off him and applied the paste to the stitched wounds and minor cuts.

*

Nothing changed in the next five days; she washed him when nature had taken its course, changed bandages and applied fresh ointment. She stayed with him when he had a fever, dried the sweat from his body and applied cold compresses to his forehead, until the giant's dreams became less restless and his face underneath the demon's mask became calm again.

Her own dreams were filled with shadow and with soldiers who looked for her in hiding or chased her. She tried to run away, but her leg held her back even more than when she was awake, a heavy and stiff thing that kept her anchored to the mud. She woke up sweating and afraid, and once she'd caught herself crying out. She burned costly candles as she lay awake, unable to face the darkness and the spectres it would bring.

On the seventh morning after her father had brought the Red Man to their farm, Ymke awoke to a thunderous roar. Her limbs tangled in her bedclothes as she tried to get up: The soldier with the red beard had been leering at her through the spy-hole and whispering vile things to her. She knew he was grinning and licking his lips, though she could only see his bloodshot, staring eyes. The image faded slowly as she clothed herself, but still she felt naked and exposed.

Her father was already in the barn. He supported the man, who sat on the edge of the cart that had been his bed. The giant's head swayed and he could barely keep his eyes open. He seemed agitated and tried to stand up, but her father gently held him down, whispering and cooing as he would to a sick animal. He shot Ymke a look and mouthed: *Get food.* She nodded and hurried away. She came back with a bowl of milk-soaked barley bread. Her father was tying a sling around the giant's massive neck to support his broken arm, and beckoned her when he'd finished. Ymke smiled as he fed the soggy bread to the giant. The patience, the little nods and the encouraging words were exactly those he had given her when she was little, though the Red Man was no child. Only once did the giant look up at her, and a feeling of immense suffering, of a body and soul in turmoil, washed over her. She shrank back, already off-kilter from her nightmare. She had to tell herself that this man, whoever and whatever he was, was nothing like the soldiers who had visited their farm and her dreams.

*

It was a good summer. Periods of sweltering warmth in which the world seemed to hold its breath were followed by exhalations of rain and thunder. The moon grew full and cut to a sliver again, and dawn broke a little later each day. Her father went on running the farm as he'd always done, but Ymke saw that the strain of harbouring the giant wore him out.

Ymke had finished her chores and sat down in the small parlour. She knew that the weather was turning even before she looked out of the window; her leg always started hurting her when rain was on the way. She sighed again and tried to rub some warmth into it. Then she got her sewing box and a folded sheet of canvas, and set to work. In time, she heard her father return to the kitchen for his midday meal, but she didn't join him. Only when the murky light started to fail did she tie the last knot and snip the thread. She stared out of the window, at the rain that mercilessly beat down on the land. In her lap lay the labour of that day: a huge pair of breeches and a shirt to match.

After a while the giant emerged, shuffling in the shadow of the shrubs and trees that bordered the house. He'd lost weight, Ymke saw, and his gait was stiff and hesitant. He made his way through the bushes to the ditch beyond to relieve himself. He was treading a path, one that had became more clearly visible in the churned up mess of wet mud and leaves. When the giant reappeared, Ymke settled something in her mind. She rose and, leaning on her good leg, slowly rotated the joint of her bad leg until she'd worked out some of the stiffness and pain. Then she went to the kitchen and opened the door.

'Hoi,' she called out. He tensed and turned round, stared at her, then caught himself and looked away. Ymke held up the shirt and trousers for him to see. She stood as straight as she could, leaning against the doorpost to take her weight off her bad leg.

'Would you come inside, please?' she called.

He had to stoop low when he entered their kitchen, and keep his head down. The stool Ymke gestured him to sit on looked ridiculously small under his bulk.

'Have you been warm enough?' she started.

'Yes,' he answered, 'and thank you for the clothing, Miss.' He ducked his head at her. 'You stitch well,' he added. His fingers involuntarily moved to the place where she'd closed the huge wound in his side.

'You're welcome. You'll need woolens for the winter, though.'

'Thank you, Miss,' he bobbed his head again, and his eyes only caught hers for a second before turning to the floor once more.

'You're among friends.' She made sure that he saw her smile.

'Friends, then, Miss,' he said, finally. He straightened his back, his head no longer bowed, his eyes not avoiding hers.

'You must call me Ymke. What's your name?' She'd noticed that it had never come up when she and her dad spoke of the man. It'd been 'he' and 'him.'

He mulled her question over. 'They shout and command and gesture. "You", they say, and, "bow before your master," and I fight for them and I bend my knee for them. When they call me, "godsdamned bloody beast," or "savage brute," I pretend that I do not understand.' He tapped the side of his head and showed her a face with slack mouth and dull eyes.

'But surely, your family -' Ymke started, but immediately knew she'd misspoken.

'Family? No, no family. There were others like me, and we gave each other names, like Crier and Lighthair. There was Kicker, who died quickly, and Swiftmace. I was Smiler, but then I got sold.'

'Do you want me to call you that?' Ymke asked.

'No,' he answered. 'To smile was to be beaten.'

Ymke shuddered. She suddenly felt the loneliness, the sheer forlornness of this giant.

'A name is the least a man should have. Take away his possessions, even the clothes on his back, and he'll still have his name,' she said. 'Since you were not given a proper name, you must take one. Let me know when you have it.'

He hesitated, then smiled. 'I will.'

They were silent for a while. Ymke rose and walked away from the fireplace, from the little warmth it gave in the afternoon. She lifted the pitcher of small beer off the shelf.

'Your leg. Were you wounded?' the giant asked.

'No, I've always been like this. Father says it happened during my birth. It doesn't bother me too much.'

When she came back with the pitcher she walked carefully, trying to not to limp.

'And how about your wounds?' she said. 'Do they hurt much?'

'Yes, some of them hurt a lot. I ignore the pain. They taught me that. To recognise the pain and move it where it doesn't hinder me. Each of these lines was a lesson in pain.' his finger moved over his face, following one of those ridged, coloured scars that spiralled around his eye socket, then wound down his cheek.

'My leg hurts so badly sometimes that I can do nothing but cry,' Ymke admitted. 'I wish then that I could cut it off.'

The giant shook his head. 'Soldiers have lost a limb and say they still feel it. Feel it hurt all the time.'

Ymke shuddered. Even when she was not in pain, she was constantly aware of her bad leg. A lifetime of living with that leg had taught her that it would not improve, and she feared it would get worse. She tried not to think of the future, as she couldn't see one in which she'd be happy.

*

The fight she had with her father that evening was short. She'd known it was coming by the way he stabbed at his food.

'Why did you let him into the house?' he had started. 'You don't know what he's capable of.' She swallowed and stared at her emptied plate.

'Do you actually know what I am capable of? If I am in any danger from him, you've brought it upon me,' she reminded him. It was true; he'd nailed down both their fates when he'd decided to save the giant from the crows and the worms.

He rose, cursing when he knocked his knee against the table top. He paced off and jerked open a drawer.

'Here.' He slammed their ledger on the table. His plate clattered and knocked over her mug. 'He doesn't eat much for someone his size, but we're already stretching the stores that were to last until harvest; we've even had to buy in some goods. You're not surprised?' She looked away.

'No, it's there, in your own hand,' he continued.

'You said we'd have a good harvest. We could always slaughter an extra cow.'

'It'll not be enough. And what of next year? Fewer calves to sell at market -' he counted on his fingers, '- less money to buy supplies, less to hire men for the next harvest. Would you have us starve? Ymke, look at me!'

'But next year he can help with the harvest. We won't need anyone else. He could even clear the far field, so we can sow it.' The far field lay full of boulders, and while they'd talked about clearing it, they'd never had the time or energy.

'Won't the neighbours wonder how we did it, just the two of us? The fields will tell their own tale to Reider Elmingha. Think, girl; we might just as well strap the giant to the plough in broad daylight, and have Elmingha take him away. And don't think he can't!'

Ymke snorted. 'Oh yes, we must be heedful of Reider Elmingha. I've heard it often enough: "Farmer Elmingha and his oldest will be here after noon with the bull, Ymke. You'd better stay in." You had me clean up the whole house, and then, when they'd left, there were muddy boot prints all over. Why are you so afraid, Pa?'

'Afraid? Without Elmingha we'd -'

'- not have this farm. I know. And we've been in his debt ever since. This is not about him though, or about the giant. This is about me. So afraid are you for me that you wouldn't even let the harvesters sleep in the barn these past few summers. Last year, you could hardly find men because of it, and you had to pay over the odds to get the harvest in. You'll have no difficulty hiding the giant; you've had plenty of practice with me.'

Her father grimaced and looked away. He unclenched his fists. His anger at her had turned upon himself.

'He's a human being, Pa,' Ymke continued, softer now, 'not an animal. You can't just keep him in the barn all the time.'

She told him about the conversation she'd had with the giant. 'He's got nobody. He's all alone and he needs us.'

'And we need him. Is that what you're saying?'

He laid a hand on her shoulder and squeezed, gently.

'I've tried to be a good father, and a mother too, when I had to. Gods know it's been an empty house for you to grow up in. There's things your mother would have taught you -' his voice cracked, but he went on, '- things I couldn't; I don't even know all I should have done.'

He sighed.

'Right.' He became brisk. 'He can have the freedom of the house. He can start helping with light chores for now. Fetch water from the well, collect the eggs. It'll save your leg.'

Ymke smiled. 'And he can sit at the fireside when he's tired, and he can tell me all he knows about the world beyond ours while I make him more clothes and teach him everything I know.'

The next morning, for the first time in weeks, Ymke didn't wake up with a feeling of dread. She had still dreamed of the soldiers, but this time when they came she'd been waiting for them, ready with the huge man behind her.

Not much later, the Red Man bowed his head and entered the parlour. He moved only when Ymke told him to, and carefully settled on a wooden chair she'd set next to the fireplace. His eyes moved over the framed prints, the heavy curtains, the few carved wooden ornaments and the painted plates above the fireplace, then found hers. His mouth was a thin line, trying to form a smile.

Ymke returned his smile and suddenly found that she didn't know what to say. The parlour had been a place to do her evening sewing, her knitting and other small chores, where she'd talk about the day with her dad, and where the occasional visitor was received. Now, this man made the room look small, and not only because of his size.

'I'll be right back,' she said, and rose, leaving the room before the tears came, tears she didn't understand.

She came back with a book clutched to her chest. She cast a quick glance at the small mirror that hung in the hall. Her eyes were still a bit red and puffy, but she hoped he wouldn't notice. She hesitated before entering the room. The giant stared out of the window, seeming lost in thought.

'This book was my mother's, and this is one of my favourite stories.' She handed him the book.

His fingers touched the heavy leather binding; moved over its gilded title, over the corners reinforced with copper; then he retracted his hand.

'It's fine, really. My father taught me to read from this book, and so I'll teach you.' She opened the book and flipped a few of the heavy vellum pages.

'These are the words that tell the story, and those are the pictures that go with them, see?'

He took the book from her and looked closely at the words, but much as he tried, the black marks remained silent to him. He turned his attention to the carefully coloured woodcut on the other page: Against a background of a walled city with steepled roofs, towers and arched windows, an army rode like a sea of helmets, bristling with spears. At the crest of this human wave rode the King, scarlet cloak and gleaming mail barely hidden by his ornate shield. The giant pointed at the things he recognized.

'That's a fine horse,' he said, and, 'Those swords are too long for close combat.'

Then his finger moved to the edge of the image, to a field of grain edged by willow trees. A peasant with a straw hat and sickle in hand peered anxiously at the passing army. A woman sat close by, binding the cut grain into sheaves. 'And there's you and your father,' the giant said.

Yes, Ymke thought, *that's us. Small figures in the margins of our lords' lives.*

They worked backwards through the book, naming the objects and people they found in the pictures, until they arrived at the first page.

'What does this mean?' she'd asked many years earlier, showing her father the plaque of red wax, with its strange marks and the crude image of a man-fish that hovered just above the name of her mother, written in swirling letters.

'Nothing,' he'd said, pushing the book back to her, 'just some play in wax to brighten up the page.'

The giant's finger hovered over the plaque, without touching it. 'The coat of arms of the Markgraf of Nyekerck. I've seen this carried into battle. Many died under it.'

Ymke cleared her throat and swallowed. 'I'll tell you the tale of Tuda and his magic pig. Do you know what a dudelsack is?'

'No.'

'I'll tell you then, and tell you how it led Tuda and his pig to fortune.'

*

The giant healed remarkably well. The scabs had fallen from even the deepest cuts, and her father thought that enough time had passed for the bones of his arm to have fused.

'And if they haven't, they never will,' he said, as he cut the bandages and padding away. Ymke flinched as the pungent odour of sweat and shed skin hit her. The giant held his arm stiffly in front of him for a moment, and rubbed it with his other hand.

'Be careful with that at first,' her father warned. 'It'll have no strength in it, and the bone may be brittle.'

'I'll be careful,' the giant promised.

Outside, heavy yellow heads of wheat were sighing in the wind, and men arrived at the farm seeking employment for the harvest. They came from afar, with packs on their backs and dirt staining their threadbare clothes and lined faces. They never came to the front of the house; Ymke dealt with them from the kitchen door. They negotiated their wages with few words and accepted Ymke's final offer with a shrug. There were some women too, one with a small child strapped to her back. She made sure to pay them the same as the men, knowing that they'd work just as hard.

Whenever the giant was done with the chores she'd given him, Ymke read him the tales from her book. He sat with his back against the wall on the window-side, so that he couldn't be seen from outside the farmhouse, and she sat next to him. She let her finger glide over the words while she read them, and then she let him point out the words. Soon he started to call out the letters and words that he recognised.

One evening, after they'd had their dinner, she showed him a wood-framed slate on which she'd written some of the words that the giant knew from the book.

'Now you try,' she said, handing him a thin stick of chalk. It almost disappeared between his thumb and finger, and his hand trembled as he painstakingly drew the letters of his first word.

'MAN,' she read. The giant beamed; he'd begun to make the letters speak. It was almost time to light the candles, and Ymke had seen his eyes flick to the window several times.

'You've done well today. Soon you'll be able to write your own tales. You can go outside, and we'll see you in the morning.'

'Remember to stay away from the other farms, and from the labourers' camp. The harvest moon is out,' her father added.

They watched him from the window, as he strode past the willows, leaped over the ditch, and was swallowed by the darkness. She'd dyed his clothes so they would stand out less against the dark of night.

As the giant's strength had grown, so had the length of time he stayed away.

Often now, he was still outside when Ymke and her father went to bed, and in the morning they would find a small pile of firewood stacked up neatly under the eaves on the south side, or some hares for the pot.

While for Ymke the coming autumn and winter were seasons of pain to live through in waiting for spring, at least this year they would not be cold or hungry, and for that she was grateful. Her father now trusted the giant and no longer feared for their safety, though he and Ymke had lived too long on their own for him to truly allow anyone else into his life. Mostly he smiled when his daughter told him what the day had brought, but that evening he was unable to lift his spirits from the gloom.

'What's the use of teaching him to write?' he asked, turning to her. 'What use is it to him? You've seen how eager he is to get outside each day. He's made for deeds, not thoughts.'

'What use?' she spat back. 'What use is it for me to know my letters? What use was it for me to have sat on your lap and learned to read? Tell me what use that is to a simple peasant girl, and I'll answer your question.'

'Add it to the list of foolish things I've done,' he said, leaving the room. 'Add it to that long list.'

The next morning, however, Ymke saw her father genuinely filled with joy, something she'd not seen for years. They'd eaten hurriedly and found the giant already gone, his pallet empty and cold to the touch. She was clearing up after breakfast when she heard her father's shout. Leaning heavily on her stick, she rushed outside.

'Ha!' her father cried out again, and grabbed Ymke by the waist. He pointed: Against the pale pink and violet sky, they saw the giant crossing the fields and leaping over ditches. He came to a halt in front of them. On his broad shoulders he carried the carcass of a deer. He exhaled as the deer landed on the ground.

'My senses have dulled and sunrise surprised me. I was slower than I thought.'

Ymke saw a ripple of worry crawl over her father's brow, but then he jerked his head and smiled. 'Come, let's not speak about it. We're grateful, aren't we? We'll butcher the deer, replenish our stores, and this evening we'll have a feast.'

While Ymke fetched buckets, some empty and some filled with water, her father propped a ladder against the barn wall and, with the giant, hoisted the deer up. Then he told the giant to keep out of the way, as he and Ymke had slaughtered and butchered together before, and they worked most quickly and efficiently in tandem. He stripped to the waist and donned a leather apron, then laid a leather roll on the ground, which soon revealed a collection of knives, saw blades, scrapers and other tools.

'Ready?' he asked, and cut the deer's throat. Ymke caught the gushing blood in a bucket, then placed a large tub underneath the carcass. Her father slit the animal's belly from groin to sternum and scooped out the entrails, which flopped with a wet sound into the tub. While he removed the beast's heart, liver and other organs, Ymke squeezed out the entrails, washed them in water and scraped them clean with a blunt knife. She'd use them as the skin for sausages.

Now and then she looked up from the dirty, smelly work and made faces at the giant, who sat against the barn wall. Then she saw that he'd slumped to one side. She rushed towards him.

They helped him up and indoors. He set one foot in front of another, yet with every step, more of his weight was carried by Ymke and her father.

'Look at your Red Man now,' he said, as he collapsed on his pallet. 'See, as he is brought down.'

He slept while they went back to work. The deer's carcass was cut up, some of the meat smoked and the rest salted. Her father took the animal's skin away a fair distance from the house, to scrape it clean, soak it and hang it to dry. Ymke sieved the blood and mixed it with salt and flour, and all that remained, apart from the bones, she chopped fine. She then threw handfuls of barley in the bucket with herbs that she'd selected from her store, and kneaded the mixture with her hands. This was the sausage filling; such things were good to eat, and the giant would need all the help he could get.

A shadow fell over her.

'Can you hand me some more of the barley?' Ymke asked.

'Pa?' She looked up. One of the labourers stood over her, his wide-brimmed hat in his hands. The others watched from a little way off.

'We've come to collect the pay owed us. We're leaving.' He had a thick accent, from the west.

'But the harvest? You can't be done already?'

'You don't understand, Miss. We're not staying here any longer. Rudalph?' He turned towards a slight, younger man in the group, who stepped forward.

'We - I was out in the night. A fair bit from the camp. Past the trees.'

'Why were you out?' Ymke asked, immediately regretting her abruptness. The man shot a quick look aside, and a young woman looked away.

'Never mind. What of it?'

'A monster, Miss. Tall as a tree, he was. His shape – it was wrong. On his head, antlers.'

'A monster, then? Tall as a tree? Ridiculous!'

The woman spoke up now. 'I saw it too. We were low in the grass, but I saw it clear as I see you. Covered in flames, so he was, leaping straight past us.'

'That's right. I covered her mouth so she wouldn't scream.' A handkerchief was tied around the hand he held up. 'She bit me.'

Ymke laughed and turned back to the older man. 'And you believe this? Telling stories because of what they were up to in the fields?' She looked round the group. The faces that met her were made of stone. The Westerner replaced his hat.

'You heard them. We're honest folk, and we put up with your father, but we'll not put up with any devilry.' He stepped forward and grabbed her arm. 'We're leaving, and we will have the pay we're owed. You give it to us, or we will take it.'

She saw the grey that flecked his stubble, the tiny hairs that grew from his nose, how the corner of his mouth trembled a little. Ymke tried to shake him off but she couldn't; his fingers were a vice. She glanced round at the barn from which she knew no help would come.

'Come, Harmen. No need for that.' The woman took his arm. 'The mistress is honest, and will give each man what he's coming to him. Won't you, Miss?' She shot Ymke a look, and Ymke nodded. The man let her go.

They followed Ymke to the kitchen and watched silently as she tallied up the wages in her ledger and counted out the coins. Outside, the man held up the purse for the others to see. The woman held back.

'I'm sorry,' she whispered. 'I hope you'll fare well, Mistress. You've been good to us.' She then joined the Westerner and the other labourers. As the group set off, Ymke stared after them, wondering what had happened to the woman's child.

'Ymke!'

Her father was running towards her. His face was red.

'There's nobody in the fields, and then I saw them all down the road. What's going on?'

'They saw him, Pa. They saw him, and they're scared. They were here to get their money, and they've gone.'

'And you paid them? How much?'

'The money owed them so far.'

'They broke word, Ymke, and there's a fine for that. You never give full wages to a word breaker. Everyone's getting their harvest in now; what do you think it costs to replace them?'

'What was I to do? Explain that what they'd seen was the giant we're hiding in the barn? Try to send them away without paying them? There was just me, Pa!'

'Damn it, Ymke.' He sighed. 'I'll be off to Reider Elmingha. Pray that he can spare some men.'

*

The vigour he'd shown when they'd unstrapped his arm had been a false dawn, and it was weeks before the giant recovered his strength again. He slept in the barn, relieved himself outside, and the rest of the time sat in the parlour. Moving around cost him considerable effort and, Ymke noticed, pain. She asked him why he didn't set aside the pain as he'd told her he could. He shook his head.

'No, Ymke. This pain, it is different. The pain of a sword's cut, of a kick, you can wrap your will around. This pain is from the inside, and my will itself is aflame with it.'

He sat on the floor, propped up on straw-filled pillows, shivering under the rough blanket he drew around him. Ymke felt his forehead and found that he had a fever. His eyes were dull, and yet he smiled as her face came near his. Despite the ridges, the spirals around his eyes and the parallel lines that combed over his cheeks, she blushed.

'Tell me a story,' he said, as he leaned back and closed his eyes.

She'd told him most of the stories from her mother's book. There was just one left; she didn't need to get the book to tell it. She knew it by heart.

'It tells of Alsigt, Prince of Suthswold,' she began, 'who fell in love with a girl carved out of wood.'

She told the giant how the prince was laughed at and mocked at court, and how he left the palace in the guise of a beggar: 'All he took with him were the rags that he wore and an old mule destined for the knacker's yard.'

The prince-in-disguise looked everywhere for the artist who had carved the portrait, hoping to find his model.

'Prince Alsigt found the artist's house in a dark and unhappy land, and he wondered how so fine a portrait could come from such surroundings. He knocked and the door opened. The girl's head appeared from the dark. She asked what he wanted. The prince wanted to answer, but he found that somewhere, in traveling the length and breadth of the country, he had lost his voice.'

Of course, the story ended well; even though he looked like a beggar the girl fell in love with him. It turned out that she herself had carved the portrait and sent it out into the world, knowing that someone, the right man, would come for her. They left that dark and dismal land, but whether they went back to the prince's country the story didn't tell. Nor did it say whether he ever found his voice again.

'But I don't think it matters. She loved him for who he was. Even as a beggar without a voice.' Ymke said.

The giant's eyes were closed, but he was awake, and she wondered what he was thinking.

'Would you leave here?' he asked.

She hesitated. 'Yes. Yes, I would.'

'Then why are you here?'

She checked herself, before he could open his eyes and see how the question had shaken her.

'We're here because my mother's family didn't approve of my father,' she said, trying to keep her voice neutral. 'And so they ran away, and bought this little piece of land with everything they had.'

'That's not what I meant,' he said. 'You speak well; you read and you write. You are not happy here, so why do you stay?'

'My father -' Ymke began, but the giant cut her short.

'Your father has known and loved other places better. You've known nowhere else, but still you don't love this place.'

His eyes were on her now. She blushed.

'Because life is not a child's fairy tale.'

The silence hung between them.

'Please,' the giant said softly, 'tell me another tale. Even if it's one for children.'

She gave him a brittle smile. She could imagine him as a child, much smaller and thinner, his first scars just healing. There'd have been no toys for him, or dolls, just swords of wood. Learning to stab and slash, evade and block. Learning to kill. She knew that his childhood had held precious little of the joy and freedom, the sheer abandon of play, that she'd taken for granted. She looked again at his face, which had become so familiar to her, and in her mind once more stripped away the scars and the ink. His mouth with the dimpled corners and full lips. His hair had grown out to a thick thatch of curls, but his cheeks were still hairless. She searched in the warm brown eyes that must have seen so much, and she found innocence.

*

With the help of Elmingha's men, the harvest was brought in. Though her father pretended otherwise, Ymke couldn't ignore that something between them had been broken. So, she was surprised when, on the cusp of autumn, he announced that they were going to have their harvest celebration that year. 'Just the three of us,' he added.

That afternoon before the harvest moon would rise, her father helped her through the stubble of the mown field to the last standing wheat sheaf. He blindfolded her and turned her around a few times, careful not to make her stumble. Then he handed her the scythe. She moved her head to feel from which direction the warmth of the sun fell on her skin, and then tried to remember where she was in relation to the wheat sheaf.

'We walked here with the sun at our backs, and were standing with the sheaf to our left. So, if I turn a quarter circle, then I should -' She swung the scythe.

'Hoi, girl! You missed the sheaf, but nearly mowed me down at the ankles.'

She knew he was joking; he would have stood well back. She tried again, and again, then she gave up guessing where the sheaf would be and mowed around her until the scythe at last found its target. A few more cuts and the scythe flew through air where the last sheaf had stood. She stood for a moment, leaning on the scythe and breathing heavily from the laughter and exercise. She removed her blindfold and looked towards the barn, shielding her eyes from the sun with her hand. The barn door was open; she waved, and thought she saw the giant waving in response.

'You did well, Ymke. A true mistress of the farm,' her father said. He'd gathered the wheat under one arm and offered her his other. They walked carefully, Ymke leaning heavily on her father's arm, and when she stumbled she laughed it off. She winced when she sat down on the wooden bench by the kitchen door, though, and let her arms bear the weight. She took the first handful of wheat from the bundle and started twisting, weaving and knotting until on her lap she held a doll about the size of a new-born babe.

In the parlour, leaves of orange, red and yellow were piled and scattered over the windowsills. She'd placed a branch of hawthorn on the small table and hung small figurines of wood and clay from its thorns with coloured ribbons. She built an altar with pinecones, whinberries and the remaining wheat ears. In its centre, on a stone plate, she placed three candles.

They ate well of the stag's meat that Ymke had prepared with thyme and bay, and of the honeyed plums she'd preserved earlier in the summer. Towards sunset they went outside. Her father had built a bonfire, and when the last sliver of the sun had sunk below the horizon, she fetched the corn doll and placed it on top. Her father said the customary prayer to the god of Winter-to-Come, and got out his tinderbox.

Winter, will you take this bride
to wed and rule the countryside
Let her seed creep 'neath the ground
There to wait, new life to found

They stood in silence for a while, basking in the heat and crackle of the flames. Ymke glanced from her father to the giant, both of them lost in thought. In the distance she saw a few flickers of orange light. They were the bonfires of the other farms, but big fires; each would have dozens of people gathered around them.

She remembered when she was little and had squealed with delight when her father lit their fire, and how she'd fed her own sticks to the flames. Her father had lifted her on his shoulder and pointed out the fires of Liwens, Kaamp, Kloster and the other hamlets that clung to the sea dike, and then of course the twin farms Sunne and Mone. They were big farms, run by Reider Elmingha and his son. She also remembered how small and pitiful their fire had looked when she got too big to be carried, and how forlorn her father looked standing there, and how one year, they just hadn't had a fire anymore.

This year's fire, she knew, would still be only a small speck of light from the other farms and the villages, but she didn't mind so much now. Her father's arm lay around her waist and her hand found the giant's hand. They stood until the fire had burnt to embers. They spoke in hushed tones about nothing of importance. Her father asked Ymke whether she was alright, whether he should fetch her a chair, and she answered that she was fine. And indeed she was, for a while at least. Finally, when she became conscious that she was leaning on her father's arm and tried to correct her stance, she nodded when he suggested they go inside.

They drank mulled wine, and ate cakes full of nuts and berries. Pine crackled in the fireplace, its burning juices giving the room a heady scent. Ymke was in the kitchen, tidying away the remains of the food, when her father began to sing a song she hadn't heard in years. The giant laughed, then her father picked up the song again. He repeated the chorus, and after a while the giant sang along with him.

And weren't we merry and filled with joy
When at last we were reunited
Our lips met each others' and hands clasped together
Our passions forever ignited

Ymke set down the empty plates by the sink, washed her hands and peered at her face in the polished surface of the large copper skillet. She smiled at the way that the curve of the copper made her face wobble and bulge. When she stepped back her reflection shrank, and when she put her hands on her hips the vague blobs of light and dark in the copper mimicked her. She looked down at her dress of black cloth, with its simple linen bodice over a white shirt.

Then she looked at the cupboard bed, and after a moment's hesitation crawled in and opened the secret door in the back panel. She reached into the hiding place, and with difficulty pulled out the small but sturdy wooden chest that waited there.

Sitting on the bed, she took out her mother's things. Her father had put them in there when she'd just been born: the things that he couldn't stand having around, but couldn't face throwing away. She unwrapped her mother's hairbrush, careful not to disturb the few golden hairs that were entangled in it, then folded the paper back and laid it aside. She took out the copper necklace with the bloodstone pendant, and the hand mirror, its silver surface now pitted with black. There was a small book with tiny print in a language she couldn't read. It was missing its spine and backboard, but must have been important for her mother to keep it. There also was a bent table knife with a bone handle, and other objects that had no monetary value but were priceless to Ymke.

Then she took out her mother's red dress, the one her father had forbidden her to wear, ever. 'I should have sold it a long time ago,' he'd said. 'Farm girls don't need dresses like that.' She held it to her face to smell the scent her mother had worn. She did not allow herself to do this often, afraid the last lingering aroma would be lost altogether. She almost put the dress back, but instead returned he other things to the chest and closed the lid.

She paused in the hall before rejoining her father and the giant. She smoothed the fabric of the red dress as much as was possible after it had been folded up for so long.

With a few quick flicks of her hands she folded her long hair behind her ears and opened the door. Her father and the giant looked at her.

'Take that off! You have no right to wear that dress!'

The words burst out of her father, and hit her painfully in her heart. Worse still was the silence of the giant, and the look on his face. She rushed out of the room, slamming the door behind her.

She stumbled through the barn blinded by tears and flung herself into the dark stall where the injured Red Man had lain months before. She buried her face in the hay, and after a while her loud cries gave way to silent sobs. She heard the giant approach, but didn't react. He waited patiently, and after a while she wiped a quick hand across her eyes and turned round.

'What!'

'I came to apologise. Seeing you in that dress - for a moment you didn't look like Ymke, but like -' he searched for the right words, sighed, and sat down next to her in the straw. His face disappeared into the shadows. His voice was low and soft, so that she had to strain to hear him.

'There were women sometimes. Rich women. Bored women. They were brought to us at night. The guards, they watched of course, and jeered and bragged afterwards.'

He stood. 'Your horse there. You admire his power, his beauty, the gloss of his coat. But he's still a beast, to pull plough and cart when commanded. To be butchered when too old or frail. To... to put out to stud in the spring.'

'You mean those women -' Ymke was unable to finish her question. A shiver ran through her, and she felt dirty wherever the dress touched her skin.

'No, they came to us just for sport. There were other women. Women like us. The best of us were taken to them. They stank when they came back; they were taut with anger and shame. I was never brought down to them, to our mothers. I wasn't good enough, and I feel lucky about it.'

Ymke imagined huge shapes shifting around in darkness and the smell of rotted straw and something else, something animal. Horror swept over her. She stood up, too quickly, and grabbed a post for support. She rubbed her thumb over the coarse, familiar wood, and drew comfort from it. She pictured herself from a distance, surrounded by the familiar objects, sounds and smells of the barn. Suddenly the door from the house opened. Ymke blinked at the sudden rectangle of light.

'Visitors! They're coming up the road,' her father said. Ymke limped towards him and his hand found her shoulder. 'You know what to do. There's just the two of us.' A soft squeeze as he ushered her in the house.

He turned to the giant, who followed behind: 'Through the barn door, hide outside.'

Ymke looked out of the kitchen window as she quickly rinsed and dried the giant's plate and mug and put them away. A one-horse trap moved past and pulled up in the front yard.

'Hooo!' she heard, and then a man jumped down. Agile, so he was young. He gave the horse a quick pat on its muzzle, then helped an older man down. It was their neighbour, Reider Elmingha of the farm Sunne, with his son Creil, who ran Mone, across the river. Ymke hadn't seen either of them in many months. They were neighbours but never visited to socialise, and her father dealt with them mainly at the market. She caught a glimpse of Creil's face as he climbed back onto the seat of the trap and settled there; it was a hard face. He'd grown into the younger image of his father. Ymke opened the kitchen door.

'Good neighbour! My cup is your cup, my bed is your bed. Share my home as though it were yours.'

It was the traditional greeting given to one's betters. The old farmer turned around, surprised to hear it issuing from the kitchen instead of the front door, as was his due. As a Lord-farmer, Reider Elmingha was not quite an aristocrat, but his status was well above that of the common rural man, and that must always be respected. Though his beard was neatly trimmed, his teeth were stained with richer fare than Ymke's household had eaten, even on that night.

'Young Ymke, isn't it? What a vision of loveliness amidst the gloom. Lead the way, young Mistress.'

She walked as evenly as possible, but was aware that the old man was staring at her legs. In the parlour, her father feigned being awoken from a light slumber, and stood up. 'Lord-farmer Elmingha. You honour us with your visit,' he said. They shook hands, but Ymke saw that Elmingha grasped her father's hand for just a bit too long.

'The honour is mine, to be met by such company.' He nodded at Ymke. 'Hasn't your daughter grown up to be quite a lady? Any man would be proud to call himself her father, I'm sure! Or her husband, though she has a bit of filling out to do yet.' His gaze fell far short of her face.

Ymke felt herself reddening. 'How thoughtless of me,' she said. 'I'll get you a drink.'

The old man laughed behind her as she left the parlour. Her father was silent. In the kitchen, she stared at the mug she was holding and steeled herself against the tears she felt welling up.

'How dare he,' she muttered, and spat in the mug. She then poured the spiced wine that still stood bubbling, and stirred it thoroughly. She took a deep breath and checked her smile in the mirror, before rejoining her father and their visitor.

'Take care. It's hot.'

He smiled at her. 'I was just telling your father here how it pleased me to spot the harvest fire burning again at this place. It's been how many years? Enough to make a woman out of a filly, anyway.'

He took a sip of his drink. 'Did you brew this? You have a way of warming an old man's bones.'

Ymke pretended not to hear the meaning behind his words and just nodded, feeling like a fool. She saw her father's hands, hidden from the other man by the table, ball into fists.

Elmingha placed his mug on the table. 'But aside from the season's greetings, I bring darker news.' He leaned forward, as if to shield his words from other ears than theirs.

'War is coming to our region again.' He nodded at that, and sat back again, his arms crossed. 'The Hertog's men are camped in front of Osinghaheerd. They're barricaded in, and they'll be able to hold the place for a while, but either the soldiers will break the siege or they'll not, and you know and I know where they'll move next.'

Ymke gasped. The stronghold of the Lord Osingha was only a couple of hours' ride away. The old farmer's hand slammed on the table.

'That's right. Here. So. That's why I've come.' He sighed and drew a mask of concern over his face.

'You've been tucked away here for years, minding your own business, ploughing your own furrow. But wouldn't you be better off amongst people, and a community that takes care of its own? You're not getting any younger, and what'll become of the girl if anything happens to you? There's a place for you on my farm, and when you can't work, I'll see you're both looked after.'

He had a point, Ymke thought; there was strength in numbers, and he was offering a security she'd never known. She thought of the giant, and in her mind he turned his head towards her and smiled. Elmingha grinned at her with stained teeth. No, not Sunne Farm. Not Reinder Elmingha. She looked at her father. He frowned, deep in thought.

'No,' he said, and rose. 'I thank you for your visit, but I must keep you no longer. Your people must be waiting for you to continue their Harvest Feast.' His formal register showed the proper deference, but Reider Elmingha pursed his mouth.

'Of course. I meant no offense or imposition.' He rose and winked at Ymke. 'A good evening to you, Mistress. I do hope to see you more often at Sunne.' He followed her father out the room. When she heard the outside door open, Ymke got up. She held back in the hall, the warmth of the parlour behind her. The farmer lingered in the doorway.

'Of course, there is the matter of the men you hired from my farm. I remind you of our terms and that I am not a lenient creditor. The next time we talk about this farm, I may not have so generous an offer.'

His voice was honey, but Ymke sensed that his manner was only a veil for his determination. Her father glared at the older man.

'I have bought this land with more than money. Our sweat and blood are in its soil. My tears are. No, you won't have it. And nor will you have us.'

'I tried. The gods know I gave you a chance.' Elmingha sighed. Then, standing back against the wall and bracing the door with his boot, he whistled. His son must have waited just out of sight. Creil barged in and threw himself on Ymke's father, pinning him to the ground.

'I've been a widower for a long time. You'd have made a decent mistress for Sunne Farm,' the old man said, bolting the door. 'After I'm gone, you'd keep that position as my son's wife.' He nodded at his son, who grinned up at Ymke. 'Alas, I will have to content myself with the land. After all, you've no family to claim it.'

Ymke's father tried to rise, but Creil's fist shot out, catching him on the cheek, then the other fist knocked his head the other way. The sound reminded her of meat being malleted. She looked from the elder Elmingha to the son, back to the father. 'Stop him!' she screamed. 'You'll kill him!'

The old farmer smiled at her, and closed his eyes.

'By the time I found them their bodies were already cold,' he recited. 'We'd missed them at our harvest celebration. Roaming soldiers must have surprised them. Such a waste!' He opened his coat and retrieved a long knife from a sheath under his arm. His son rose, laughing, with his fists bloodied. As he turned to her, his laughter caught in his throat. He stumbled backwards, and his father, mouth opened wide, stared past him, past Ymke. She heard a low rumbling behind her, and a huge hand carefully but quickly pushed her aside. The giant leapt at Creil. His huge arms locked around Creil's head, around his torso. The young man was tall and strong, but no match for the giant. With a sickening crunch, Creil fell, his arm torn from its socket and his head at a horrible angle. Ymke saw the young man's grin, now fixed on his face. The giant lunged at the dead man's father. The old man's knife glanced off thick skin as the giant's huge hand caught his head and rammed it against the wall. The farmer crumpled to the floor, leaving a flower of blood, brains and splinters of bone. The giant dropped to his knees and let out a roar that froze Ymke's blood. He clasped both gory hands and raised them above his head, then the knot of his fists once more collided with flesh. The old man's lifeless limbs jumped up under the impact, then dropped down again.

The giant stayed on the floor. His breath came in hacking bursts and his shoulders were shaking. Ymke realised that was crying. A groan came from the floor; her father stirred. Ymke knelt and steadied him.

'Hold still,' she urged. 'Let's see how bad it is.'

'I'll live,' he said, bubbles of blood and spittle welling

from his mouth. She helped him move a little, so he could prop himself against the wall. He looked around at the broken bodies of Reider Elmingha and his son, the gore on the walls and the floor tiles, and the giant's shaking back. He grasped his daughter's shoulder and pulled her towards him. 'See to our friend.'

She nodded and rose. She didn't know what to say, but hoped the words themselves wouldn't matter.

'Hoi,' she said, and laid a hand on the giant's shoulder. He shook it off and rose. He fumbled with the door's catch, slippery under his bloody fingers, finally opened the door and stumbled out. Very soon, his running form was swallowed by the dark.

'Wait!' Ymke called after him. The night's chill cut through the thin red dress, and after waiting a while she closed the door. She stepped over the dead men as if they were fallen trees, and helped her father to the kitchen, where she filled a bowl with water to clean his cuts. The bruises and swelling would take many days to disappear, but he seemed to have no broken bones.

'What about -' she said, nodding towards the hall. Her father sighed.

'Let me have some strong wine first to dull the pain, then we'll attend to them.'

They wrapped the bodies in sack cloth, dragged them outside and dug a deep hole. They scrubbed the blood from the hall floor, cleaned the wall as much as they could, and moved the hall cabinet in front of the remaining stains. Her father dealt with the horse last of all, leading it to the road and slapping its flank to send it, confused but biddable, on its familiar route home. Then, at last, they went to bed.

Ymke listened to the night, hoping for the giant to return and fearing that the Elmingha family would come looking for them. Should someone come from Sunne, as they must, it had been agreed that Ymke would excuse her father's absence - still sleeping off the Harvest cheer, she'd say. She would be surprised the men had not come home, but tell the messengers, wide-eyed, of Reider Elmingha's warning that brutal soldiers once again roamed the countryside.

*

The sun was well into its ascent when she sat up, suddenly wide awake as the horrors of the night washed over her. She steadied herself by clinging to her everyday routine, slinging her blanket over her shoulders to keep some warmth inside of her aching bones. When she went to the kitchen to wash and make breakfast, she found his letter. She already knew what it would say before she picked it up.

My friends, she read, *I cannot stay. I tried to be a farmer, but the night showed me that war is in my blood. I am made to fight, not to grow things or to build them. You gave me a home and were my family. I won't forget you.*

Ymke observed that the quill had been clumsy in his large hand, but wielded with the sureness with which he did everything. He'd signed it with a scrawl that she could not have deciphered if she hadn't known what it said. She smiled at it, even as her heart broke.

'Alsigt,' she said to herself. 'So, at least you left with a name.'

She read those few lines again, then very slowly she folded the letter and finally began the tasks that must be done every morning on a farm. It was well past noon when she saw horsemen coming, and she was ready to greet them with a smile, and then surprise, when they asked about their master, the farmer Elmingha.

That evening, Ymke and her father talked. Ymke was resolved to hold her life together, while her father sounded as defeated as he looked. Both his eyes were blackened, and his cut lips and swollen cheeks made speaking difficult.

'As the fox will go after the chickens, they'll be back,' he said.

'And we'll tell them what I told them before, Pa. That it must have been the soldiers, from Osinghaheerd.'

'I didn't think you'd believe Elmingha's tale. There's no soldiers at Osinghaheerd. No, his people will search the ditches and the fields and talk it over. When the farmer and his son don't come home, they'll know we have something to do with it. Then, whether we acted in defence or malice will not make a difference to them.'

*

From the box of the cart Ymke looked back until the farm had disappeared from view. First they drove through fields she knew, past trees that she'd seen bud in spring and bare their branches in winter. Lines of flame crept over the fields. The harvest safely indoors and the Harvest Feast over, farmers and farm hands had returned to the fields with sore heads and torches to set fire to the stubble.

She glanced at her father. His face was every hue between dark blue and yellow, but his back had straightened, and he was smiling. Then she knew: He did not regret leaving the farm behind. He had cast off the guise of the farmer, and a man emerged who had not been seen since before she was born.

Gradually, all that was familiar disappeared, and she entered a world that was unknown to her; the flat fields of clay gave way to sandier grounds, and the road disappeared into the shadow of huge, dark pines. They were going south, though slowly, winding their way over smaller roads, going east for a while and then the other way again, just in case they were looked for. They had not wanted for food or lodgings; her father had knocked on the doors of men who'd been surprised to see him, then hugged him and welcomed them in. These friends had introduced them to their wives, but said nothing more when they saw the quick shake of her father's head. He was a new man, or rather the man he'd once been, but that man was almost a stranger to her. Only when she'd been packed off to bed, with love but insistence, and she strained her ears to overhear the conversation of her father and his old friends, did she find out how little she'd really known of him.

*

The hamlet they drove through was a smouldering ruin of brick and wood. They'd passed the people who had lived there. Their belongings, along with their old and their youngest, were piled on a few carts drawn by skin-over-bone mules and stone-faced men. Their women cried without tears and warned them off the road they were taking.

Her father had thanked them and given some coins, then urged the horses onward. Now they'd stopped.

'If you insist, you must go. I'll wait here,' her father said. He drew the horsehair blanket tightly around himself, and settled back. Ymke crossed the uneven ground between the trees as fast as her bad leg would allow, and she leaned heavily on her walking stick. Soon her breath came out in ragged bursts, and she grew warm enough to throw back her shawl. She smelled the battlefield before she saw it. The smoke, of course, had been visible for some distance, but nothing prepared her for the stench of blood and sweat and the muck of the soldiers and their mounts. The field must once have grown crops, but it was churned up beyond recognition by the thousands of feet and the ironclad hooves of two armies. And as she watched from the shade of the trees, in the midst of the battle she saw him.

She knew it was him, her Red Man, and no other. He towered over the battlefield, making the soldiers around him look like children. He swung his huge arms and men fell to his left and to his right, and she saw the tide of battle turn around him. Which side he was fighting for, she could not tell, nor did she care.

She turned back the way she had come. Her father lifted his head, and she nodded. That was all he needed to know. She climbed onto the box next to him, and they set off towards the next city and the world beyond. Ymke drew her pack close to her. In it were her books, her writing things and her mother's red dress.

In her head were all the things her mother, her father, and the Red Man had taught her.

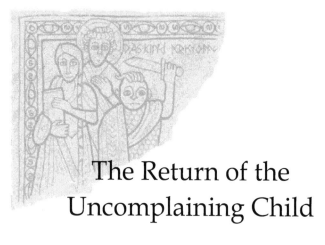

The Return of the
Uncomplaining Child

I write all of this down because that's what I do: I write. I
can't resist it, and have kept a journal from the moment I
left the grim lands of my youth. And when times are lean,
nobody seems to have need of a scribe, and the cost of ink
and paper are a burden on my purse, what of it? I just cut
my quill sharp and write small.

Nobody will read this, though. I'll make sure of that.
I'll probably burn it, to protect Kaila, Sebastien and myself.
I'm damn well going to tell the tale first though, if only to
amuse myself and relive those days in Otasring, where I
met Kaila. She's sitting at the window, edging her sword.
She looks up and smiles at me. I smile back, though I know
that soon we'll each go our own way.

*

There's another document that'll never be read: the
manuscript that sits on my desk now, tightly rolled and
sealed, mocking me. Writing down Father Folkhert's
memories, arranging them chronologically (and let me tell

you, that was a chore in itself; he remembered much but was old and easily muddled), then turning them into readable prose: All for nothing. I might have to burn that one too, as it'll do me no good if the Wheelies get hold of it.

Father Folkhert really, truly, felt awfully sorry for me when I told him about the visit I'd had from the Alabaster Branch of the Brotherhood of the Wheel. He wanted to compensate me for my labour, he said, but I had to understand that he couldn't possibly just pay me, now the Brothers had banned the book. Instead, he gave me an extravagant cloak, which he suggested I could wear when meeting wealthy clients, and of course I was always welcome to visit him if ever I was in distress.

Then he introduced me to Brother Walther who, allegedly, was there to help him with errands and odd jobs. Brother Walther ignored my hand, and told me, smiling through clenched teeth, that the Father was tired and I ought not to take up more of his time.

'Ymke, dear,' the old man said, clasping my hands, as I bade him farewell. 'Come again, won't you? I did so enjoy our little chats!'

I walked without glancing back until I'd passed under the Guderian Arch, that oppressive example of Otasring masonry, where I knew that the old Father could no longer see me from his little stone bench. I eyed the cloak that he'd given me; it was expensively made and richly decorated, but also mouldy and threadbare. I couldn't understand why the old man would give me this. These things just didn't leave the Brotherhood, and only the First

Brothers would wear or even own cloaks like it. I wouldn't be able to sell off even a moth-eaten specimen like this as a curiosity without raising the suspicion that I'd filched it. As for wearing it – no.

After crossing Guderia's Mile with its long row of narrow, identical granite-walled houses, I dived into the warren of streets where people's homes were narrower still, crammed together sideways and upwards. Everyone lives cheek by jowl in Otasring, on the flat top of that enormous rock, the Otasfaust.

I think that the Otasringar are shaped by the ancient forest that surrounds the rock, just as those giant tree trunks made their mark on me when I guided my horse between them just a few years ago. There's very little green in the city, and what trees and shrubs there are get snipped and pruned carefully. It's as if the Otasringar fear the forest so much that they've hewn a culture from granite, with high walls and small windows, to keep it out. Yet with those looming, stark buildings and those winding streets, they've ended up living in an echo of the very forest they sought to escape. The architecture of Otasring is reflected in turn in the people who dwell within her walls: Sturdy folk with long limbs and angular features.

I'd walked faster than I should to keep up with the movement of the crowd, and I was leaning heavily on my stick.

'Verzeihung!' I mumbled. The dour-faced man I'd bumped into nodded curtly and was swallowed by the crowd. I could no longer ignore the burning of my hip, and when I spotted an inn ahead of me I limped the last few yards and tumbled inside.

'Gods rot me!' I said as I collapsed on one of the wooden benches. The words rolled over my tongue like old but seldom visiting friends. I don't curse often, but when I do, I do so in the low, guttural tones of my youth.

'And they will, in the end.'

The traditional response came unexpectedly. I looked around the dimly lit inn. Two elderly women had taken seats at the one small window, and were trying to get the attention of the innkeeper. Behind me, underneath the antlers of a giant elk, sat a young girl. She gave me a quick, one-sided grin and raised her tankard.

'You're a long way from home, aren't you?'

'As are you,' I smiled back at her. Her Hunergou was heavily accented, and she was too dark to be from the north.

'You speak Hunergou well,' I said. She was older than I'd first thought, but very small. Powerfully built, though.

'You learn fast in the barracks. I fought up in the north.' She held my gaze for a second. 'I know you'll not ask me which side.'

'Indeed. It doesn't matter,' I said. This, too, was traditional for us northerners. Between truces and open hostilities the war at home had gone on for decades, and we common folk were interested less in whether this or that lord was winning, than in getting the harvest in without being trampled, robbed or killed.

'Good. And with that out of the way -' she slipped off her bench and moved over to my table. She sat down and stuck out her hand.

'I'm Kaila.'

'Ymke,' I said. I was ready to flinch but her grip was gentle.

For a moment there was silence between us. I felt myself go red and hoped she wouldn't notice in the sparse light. I stared at the table. It was of heavy oak, darkened with the beer and wine slops of decades and smoothed by thousands of elbows. My finger traced the initials that had been carved in the wood by generations of patrons.

The innkeeper, dirty rag slung over one shoulder, had come up and cleared his throat, saving me from further embarrassment. I ordered a small beer for myself, and a refill for Kaila, and asked her whether she'd eaten yet. Her fingers made the fluttering movement of moths flying from an empty pouch: Breakfast would have to be on me, but I could do with the company, and despite my own impending insolvency it was worth the price. I asked the innkeeper what he would recommend. I didn't know why I bothered, as the Otasringar breakfast varies as little as its architecture. He sighed and nodded at the sign behind the bar. 'Breakfast,' it read in the cramped and angular script of Otasring, 'Sausages on bread. All day.'

'Well, bread and bangers for us both then,' I said.

'Ehm, make that three, please.' Kaila gave me an apologetic smirk. I raised an eyebrow, and she nodded to our side, at the doorway.

'Wait!' She crossed her arms in front of her on the table and settled down. I didn't have to wait too long.

The boy who lurched into the doorway had unruly blond hair, thin cheeks and a very sparsely fluffed chin. He had a wide-eyed look of concern on his face and a pouch in his hand. He peered through the gloom until he spotted the two old women. He grinned and lumbered over to them.

'M'ladies, would either of you have lost her purse?'

I looked at Kaila. She winked and put a finger to her lips. 'Meet Sebastien, my minion, apprentice, and sometimes partner,' she whispered. 'Watch!'

The womens' eyes darted from the purse in the boy's hand to one another, and their hands flew to their belts. One of them retrieved a pouch; the other came up with nothing but a gasp.

'You're in luck, so you are,' Sebastien said, handing over the purse. 'This part of town is full of ruffians, as you'll well know. Best count your money, and make sure it's all there.'

The woman shook her head in dismay and her lips moved wordlessly, berating herself. She poked through the contents of her purse, then a smile formed. 'It's all there, young man. I'm ever so thankful.'

'Och, not at all,' he said, picking up the coins she held out to him.

He spotted Kaila and sat down at our table, as inconspicuously as he could. The ladies glanced over to him once or twice, and he beamed them a guileless smile that slid off his face like water the moment he turned back to us. Kaila beckoned the innkeeper, held up three fingers and circled them over our stone tankards.

'That's the bill settled. Drink up, Ymke, to your good health.'

I was still halfway down my first tankard, and raised it in salutation.

Soon, with bread, sausage and small beer in front of us, we were complaining about the noise in the city and the rudeness of its inhabitants, as strangers meeting in foreign places always do.

'And the clothing. I'm not sure I'm too fond of these,' said Sebastien, eyeing his short-sleeved tunic with its diagonal thunderbolt motifs. He lifted a leg above the table and showed off a stocking with leg windings.

I laughed. 'It took me a long time to get used to these long, woollen dresses, but I like them.' And I do. They're less cumbersome than they look, and warm, and when I walk slowly, they hide the unevenness of my gait. I like that they're simple, only decorated with a broad, rune-covered girdle.

'Other women would see how filthy and frayed the hems get and say, 'Don't let the hem drag like that. You're not indoors, are you?' I don't really care; back on the farm we didn't have the luxury of clean, whole clothes.'

Kaila shrugged. 'There's enough to like. Just use what you want and leave out what you don't.' She was wearing a man's tunic, but had tied it with the rune girdle. She'd studded her tunic on the back and front with plaques of metal and wood. They were each the size of a fist, and my eyes glided over the runes and the engravings of bears and other creatures that covered them.

'Yes, I'm short!' Kaila laughed.

'What?' I said, and clapped a hand to my mouth. 'I mean... I didn't...'

'I don't mind. I am short, but I'm fit and strong, and fast. I've got stamina too.' She winked. 'People underestimate me, and that's an advantage when working as a private guard or armed escort. Nobody expects someone like me to come between them and a successful theft, kidnapping or assassination.'

I raised an eyebrow, but her matter of fact tone told me that she wasn't making any of it up.

'You don't know of anyone looking to hire a strong arm and a swift sword, do you?' She bent towards me, lowered her voice: 'Perhaps you'd like to have someone bumped off?'

I must have looked horrified, because she laughed.

'I'm joking,' she said. 'We don't go quite as far as that; we like to think we're more or less on the side of the angels.'

I smiled sheepishly, suddenly feeling like the bumpkin I had been when I first came to Otasring.

'Needs must, I suppose,' I said, quickly. 'And I have to admit, at times I've wandered off the straight road myself.'

'You?' Kaila cocked an eyebrow.

I told them how, new to Otasring, I had found myself caught in its apprentice system. You can't get work as a scribe unless you're registered, and you can't get registered until you've apprenticed with a master scribe. And he, always a he, signs your recommendation papers. However:

'It only took a week of eating slops in the word mines to know that the master scribes were running a scam. They've got halls set up, crammed to the rafters with writing benches, where apprentices grow old and permanently stooped. There's no reason for the scribes to sign any recommendation while their apprentices bring in the money in trade for a bowl of thin soup. The other apprentices just shrugged when I asked them about it. Either they were poor and happy with their bowl of soup, or they were a wayward member of a rich family, given a choice between becoming a scribe and getting a stipend, or joining the army.'

'So, how did you get your recommendation papers?' Sebastien asked, giving the ladies at the window seat yet another sunny smile.

'It turned out to be ridiculously simple in the end. I wrote a letter of recommendation myself, and then signed it with a made-up name. If anyone suspected, nobody cared. That was four years ago, and since then I pay my taxes as a fully qualified, registered scribe.'

Perhaps it was this, as much as anything else, that made Kaila and Sebastian trust me.

'So, those scribes. Any of them you want to have bumped off?' Kaila said. 'I'll cut you a deal. Two for the price of one.'

I snorted into my beer. 'Not the scribes. And death can't come cheap, even at a discount. But if I had the funds -' I leaned over the table and lowered my voice still further: 'I'd start with the Alabaster Branch of the Brotherhood, and end with that damned Child himself, if he'd not been burnt two-score years ago.'

'Ah, the Uncomplaining Child,' she whispered, her use of his proper name sarcastic in the extreme. 'We've had our run-ins with the Wheelies ourselves. How did you get mixed up with them?'

'Well, I had this old man come to me; he'd been tutor to the Child's family, back when Kristjoffel was just a child with a small "c." Knew the boy well, loved him to bits, and he wanted to put down his recollections of the boy's origins and family. Everything from sweet stories about his boyhood – the usual even-as-a-toddler-he-was-special stuff – to the lineage of the family, and how "that flow of seed made them the natural fount to produce a saint." Yes, those were his words. I felt lucky to get the job, and I was promised good money and a percentage of the sales.'

'But?' Sebastien asked. He'd also stuck his head close to ours.

'But,' I explained, 'while Wheelies like their stories about their saint, the Brotherhood is possessive about his life story and how it's told. The ramblings of an old man are not welcome, most definitely not if they're true. So they shafted me and, as I just found out, put a guard on the old man. And all I got was this cloak.' I showed them the folded piece of cloth.

'It's priceless,' Sebastien said, taking up a corner between thumb and fingers. 'Literally. Nobody would take it off your hands, legally or otherwise. There may be something that can still be saved from this fiasco, though. There's power in words.'

'That's what they're afraid of. And if I found a publisher stupid enough to print it now, my life wouldn't be safe. Word will have gone round.'

'What he means,' Kaila said slowly, catching on, 'is that you have detailed information about the life of Kristjoffel, which is known to only a few. I know just how we can turn that knowledge into money. Sebastien, do the thing!'

Sebastien closed his eyes. He lowered his shoulders, stretched his neck a little and folded his hands. He leant forward slightly, his face upturned. In doing so, he entered a shaft of morning light that had been making its way across the table. Then he opened his eyes and looked at me. They were wide and blue, and filled with the purest innocence and pain; the pain of a child who has just learned that everyone dies in the end. His lips were pursed ever so slightly, as if he were trying to control the desire to cry out. One tear formed in the corner of an eye and rolled over his cheek.

'I'll be damned. It's Kristjoffel!' I whispered. His portrait could be found everywhere in the homes and temples of the devout. The first ones were painted by those who'd known him, allegedly, then copied by less deft hands. The expression was always there: That of a boy who knows of the suffering of all humanity and the meaning-lessness of his own impending death, bound to a wheel and set alight. A boy who bears it stoically, except for the one tear he sheds for his poor old mother.

The accuracy of Sebastien's impersonation was unsettling, yet I couldn't help feeling bereft when he blinked and made it disappear. I caught myself thinking about what would happen if Kristjoffel were to actually, physically return from the dead. For one thing, I'd have no difficulty selling the book, if the Child himself were there to endorse it. *And what if...*

'It can never work,' I dismissed my own thoughts. Kaila, however, had already read the temptation in my face, and knew just how to play on it.

*

I want to say here and now that I regret involving the old man. Father Folkhert was our dupe, and he had the most to lose, in particular his illusions about the boy he'd cared for and lost. He had ceased working for the Child's family before the boy's visions began in earnest, and before the cult started. 'Family obligations of my own,' he'd claimed, but said no more. Maybe he saw what was coming: When the Child was killed and his followers were rounded up by the dozen, he was far enough removed to escape being wheeled to death himself.

I felt that he owed me, though, and without him we could never have made it work. It would be his belief that made Kristjoffel real.

We decided that Kaila and Sebastien should quit their lodgings and move in with me for the time being. It would save the money which we sorely needed, as our plan would take time to bear fruit, and we wouldn't be free to do any other work. Not that I lived in a palace, but Sebastien made himself comfortable enough under the table, and my bed was big enough for Kaila and myself. We talked long into the night, sketched out a plan between bursts of Sebastien's giggles and Kaila's deep, gurgling laughter, and discussed our first actions in detail. Eventually, though, no more useful thoughts came, and it was time to sleep.

'Are you sure the person who'll have the most important role in this shouldn't have the comfort of a real bed?' Sebastien asked from underneath his table.

'Good night, Sebastien,' Kaila said, and closed the door of my small bedroom behind her.

*

It was still early morning when I returned to Father Folkhert's house, and I was glad to have had the walk over to properly waken up. As was his custom, he sat on the ancient stone bench underneath the pear tree beside his front door. He sat there most of the day, summer and winter, watching over Guderian Square where the children played, talking with neighbours, vendors and anyone else who passed by and would spare him a word. He greeted me as an old friend, not someone he'd dismissed the day before, and I wondered whether he'd forgotten about it.

I rubbed my bad hip as I sat down on the bench beside him.

'We'll have rain later today,' Father Folkhert said, seeing me wince. 'I feel it in my knees and wrists.'

I glanced round. 'Where is...?'

'Brother Walther? He'll be back shortly with building supplies. As he's to live with me, it was decided that the house needs,' the old man breathed in and grabbed in the air for the words, 'restorative works.'

My eye caught the peeling paint and cracked plaster of the house's facade. They were only an indication of the state of it on the inside, as I'd discovered the one time I'd been indoors. 'At my age you don't need much,' he'd assured me when he saw my concerned look. I had gathered most of the material for the book on this bench, though he'd taken us to the comfort of the square's small bakery a few times when he noticed I was in pain.

'Ymke,' the old man said, laying a hand on my arm and waiting until he had my full attention, 'It seems I'm not permitted to discuss... certain things.' He glanced round.

'I understand,' I nodded, 'we'll not talk of it. It's fine.'

'No. No. It is not. I have survived war and plague and all manner of lunacies. And now I have reached this great age, and instead of respect I get a nursemaid! Oh, I loved the Child dearly, and not a day goes without a reminder of him, but they... they...'

He stood up and looked around as if to single out a target for his scorn, but as quickly as it had flashed up, that heat died down again. All that was left was an old man standing in front of a ramshackle house with a young, lame woman at his side. Then, on cue, our attention was drawn to a commotion across the square.

It emanated from the junk shop, which sold the usual selection of tatty stuffed birds, rusty tools, disbound books and other goods of unknown origin and no purpose. To the annoyance of Father Folkhert, the place also had a thriving trade in fake relics of the Child.

'You want to know what they had on display last week? Kristjoffel's skull. No, not skull. Skulls. They had two of them! And both of them sold, to the same man. What is wrong with these people?'

A group of people was now milling in front of the shop's window, and others hurried over at their beckoning. Then a slender shape in cloak and cowl burst from the door opening, scattering the folk in his path, running towards us. The shopkeeper emerged behind him.

'Halt! Thief!' As they say, the bigger the crowd, the slower it moves. Before people had taken heed of the shopkeeper's cries and the mob was halfway across the square, the thief had swept up to us and knelt down. He reached into the folds of his cloak.

'This belongs to you,' he said, thrusting his hand at Folkhert. The wooden object was in the old man's hands before he could think about taking it. He stared at it, then looked up and raised one hand.

'Stop!' he commanded. I saw an echo of the man he'd once been, the man who'd taught a living god. And the shopkeeper and his mob did stop, just like that, and they looked on as the old man returned his attention to the object: A crude hinged box with metal bands. The lid had a boar carved on it, with tusks of ivory. He turned it over and over in his hands.

'It certainly shouldn't be in that place, young man,' he said to the thief, who still knelt at his feet. Under the cowl I saw Sebastien's nose and chin. Kaila had said that Sebastien would introduce himself to the old man, but not when or how. She said it was better that way, that my reactions would be more real.

'This is a relic,' said the old man, 'But it is not as the relics of the other faiths. They coat their most precious objects with gold to hide the simplicity within. But as with the Child, simplicity itself is the message that we should imitate.'

His words unwittingly hit exactly on what we were trying to do. I blushed, but he did not notice.

The old man fumbled with the catch, and the box opened. I peeked over his shoulder, pretending curiosity about its contents. He smiled and held it up to me.

'Jewels beyond price.'

It had taken some effort to find the right sort of box, and have it decorated. Then we'd damaged it. The real thing had probably burned along with the Child, his family and his home. We trusted that the dimming of memories and a helping of wishful thinking were enough for it to work. *Jewels beyond price.* Kaila didn't tell me where they'd procured a full set of baby teeth, and I didn't dare ask.

The shopkeeper made a small noise in his throat to remind us that he was still there. Father Folkhert waved him away.

'I'll pay for it, of course. Talk with Brother Walther. Name your price. And you, young man,' (to Sebastien, still kneeling at his feet), 'you must be rewarded. But how could you know? I thought everything had burned. There's so little left of his.'

'Oh, but you mustn't think of it. You've given me so much already. Given us all so much, I mean.' Crafty kid, misspeaking and correcting himself. I noticed his voice was gentle and empathic, different from the one he used with Kaila and myself. 'My reward will be the glow in your heart.'

'The glow in my heart,' Father Folkhert muttered, and leaned forward. A memory tugged at him, of a child's turn of phrase. 'The glow in my heart.'

Sebastien rose and pushed a lock of hair away, allowing the cowl to fall back. At that exact moment the sun broke through the clouds. I still wonder whether that was coincidence or expert timing. Sebastien did the thing; his angelic expression was at full tilt as he looked down upon us both, and to my horror, I still felt the awe. I couldn't bear to look at the old man, but I felt him tense beside me.

'Kristjoffel?' he said, his voice wavering.

'Right,' a harsh voice snapped. 'whatever it is, that's enough of it.' Brother Walther shouldered through the crowd that still stood around us, stepped right in front of Sebastien, and hid him from the old man's sight. His eyes, though, were directed at me. He folded his arms and made his biceps swell.

'What are you doing here? He's no longer your client.' Then he glared at the old man. 'And as for you, can't I go on an errand without you getting up to all manner of foolishness? Time for your afternoon nap.' His coal shovel hand crooked under the thin armpit and he dragged the old man inside. Father Folkhert kept pointing, and his cries turned from surprise to joy.

'Kristjoffel? My boy, is it really you? Kristjoffel the Child?'

Before I could decide whether to intervene or not, he was gone. The crowd, which had also stood by as the old man was bundled away, looked at the boy, whispered to each other, looked again and nodded or frowned.

Sebastien himself slipped away between the buildings before they thought of touching him. I found myself alone with the crowd, and had to feign surprise and elation with the rest of them until I also could get away.

*

We had planted the seed and, watered by gossip, the Return of the Uncomplaining Child was in bud. Kaila would prove herself to be the master gardener who brought it into bloom. I, meanwhile, was to stick as much to the square and the old man as I could, acting as her eyes and ears.

We didn't hear Sebastien sneaking back into my home the next morning. It was still dark when he knocked on the bedroom door, and we woke up just enough to hear him tell us that everything had gone according to plan. He was fast asleep underneath his table when we emerged in the morning light.

'Look at him,' Kaila whispered to me. 'When he sleeps you can see a bit of the child he was.'

As I slipped past him on my way out to see Father Folkhert, I looked at him again and wondered: Had he ever been a child? Or were the hours between nod and wake the only trouble-free ones in his life?

*

Despite the rain, a small crowd of people had gathered around Father Folkhert by the time I arrived. Brother

Walther had tried to send them away, claiming that the old man was gravely ill after the previous day's events, but they only returned with broth and a greater insistence upon seeing him. Maybe they feared he'd die before they could secure an audience. Eventually, Brother Walther gave in, knocked up an awning above the little stone bench and brought the old man out. His dramatic recovery added further lustre to the miracle in the making, so Brother Walther inadvertently proved the old adage right: You also need dung to make plants grow.

Brother Walther was dripping with rain and resentment when he saw me, and quickly moved to occupy the bench before I could sit down. Folkhert squeezed closer to him, freeing up a corner for me. I thanked him with genuine gratitude. My leg had become a column of pain, and on my way over I'd had to sit down and rest several times.

'Goodwife Kunelore,' Folkhert smiled and beckoned an old woman from the crowd. The cloak she wore draped over her humped back was threadbare, and the patina had worn off the circlet she wore above her brow, revealing the plain iron underneath. She pressed a small loaf of bread into his hands.

'For the poor,' she said, even though the thinness of her face and hands revealed her own meagre meals. 'Is it true? Has the Child returned?'

'It is true. He visited me last night.' The old man settled to tell his story. It was well rehearsed by this time, though he unwittingly stuck fairly close to the scenario we had prepared for him. Under the cover of night and bad weather, when even strumpets and robbers were indoors,

Sebastien had gone to the old man's house. He knew which window at the back of the house had rotted woodwork and a catch that would easily come away, and once inside he knew where Father Folkhert slept.

'He sat on the edge of my bed and woke me, as he would do half a lifetime ago, when he couldn't sleep for the demons that plagued him. I thought, maybe he is a waking dream, or a cruel trick of my ageing mind. I was about to call for Brother Walther, when his hand on my mouth told me that he was there, in the flesh. Then he spoke, and I knew for certain that here, before me, sat the Child Returned.'

Sebastien and the old man had talked for a few hours, sharing memories I'd primed him with, cribbed straight from the book that the Brotherhood had tried to destroy. He told me later that the small details were the most powerful. He'd reminded the old man of the dandelions in the courtyard of their classroom, and how they'd blown the clocks away. 'We both got tears in our eyes, Ymke. Blowing dandelion clocks; can you believe it?' I could, of course. Such were the small things I missed most of all from the farm I had grown up on, and had to abandon.

Sebastien told Father Folkhert that only a few years earlier, the memories of his previous life had started to come back to him, alongside a pull towards Otasring which he found increasingly hard to resist. 'You must have been the exact age at which your previous form was taken from us,' calculated the old man, 'and it was home beckoning you. Oh! I am so glad that you are here. Please tell me that we will meet again!'

'Of course. I will return very soon. I wish also to manifest to my flock. There are so many people out there who need me.'

The old man beamed as he narrated the night-time visit of the Child to Goodwife Kunelore, as he beamed again when he told it to half a dozen others. One thing, however, he left out.

'Never forget the glow in your heart,' Sebastien had told him as he disappeared into the night. Kristjoffel would appear to many, but these words should reassure the old man that he occupied a place in Kristjoffel's heart that no-one else could usurp.

*

I stayed longer at the old man's side than we had planned. The shadows had pushed what dim sunlight there was past the rooftops, and someone had draped a woollen blanket around Father Folkhert's shoulders. We'd eaten from the plain food that people had brought, and it was only when someone hung a lantern from the pear tree that I left for home. What kept me at the old man's side was not his own story, but what the people told him in exchange. They laid their whole lives out before him, and only then did it become clear to me how hungry these people were for a symbol of hope.

'They don't even know if Kristjoffel's the real thing,' Kaila said over her cold dinner. 'It's a joke, really. It's all about appearances. I heard that the harvest failed a couple of years ago. They insisted on holding the Great Gourd

Festival though, so what did they do? They carved vegetables from wood and covered them in paint. And told everyone that the bloody things were real, because to stop pretending would mean to stop believing that the gods are always looking out for us, that our rulers are not corrupt and that the sewers never overflow.'

I sat back and toyed with the remains of my dinner. 'That may be true, but we all have to believe in something. Kaila, you believe in the strength of your arms, and Sebastien believes in his swiftness and wit. I believe... I believe that there's something that is greater than each of us, or all of us together. And not everyone feels strong enough inside to believe in themselves, so what is the harm in giving them something to hang their hopes on, even if it's for a short while?'

'Especially when it'll fill our purses?' Sebastien added, practical as ever. 'We bring hope to the little people, they'll bring us the big people, and the big people will happily pay for the privilege of being fleeced.'

And though it took a while for the big people to come, word about the miracle got around, and the curious and the needy streamed from the wide lanes and forgotten corners of Otasring to the square. In less than a week, I was sitting in front of Folkhert's house, organising the growing throngs of the faithful into something resembling a queue that stretched a third of the way through the quarter towards the Guderian Arch. Only the most faithful were admitted to the Presence of the Child: Those who displayed that faith in monetary form, and the lost souls who I felt would genuinely benefit from an audience. I'd suggested slipping coins into the pockets of the poor, thinking that small miracles would help spread the word, but Kaila dismissed the idea. We didn't want to have the square overrun with all the down-and-outs of the city; our aim was to have the Child remind the better-off of their charitable duty.

Those who didn't get a private audience with the Child had to make do with the group blessings that Sebastien bestowed from a platform erected on the square, courtesy of the Carpenters' Guild. It seemed nobody went home terribly disappointed, as everybody got a glimpse of the Child, and could have a stroll around the market that had assembled itself on the square. Brother Walther gave me no further trouble once he had set himself the task of collecting rent from the stallholders. He also skimmed the donations for the poor that were brought to the Child, but so of course did we. Even the junk shop opposite was doing a brisk trade in hastily assembled relics. The proprietor did have to be dissuaded from selling any further skulls or other bones of the Child, as that would have defied both taste and logic.

We were very careful to keep the Child's appearances frequent enough to draw the crowds, but short enough to keep their appetites whetted. He usually came from Father Folkhert's house and disappeared inside again, giving most people the idea that he stayed there permanently, a notion Father Folkhert did not correct. Some figured, more accurately, that he materialised in the house's small rear garden, and a few had awaited his coming on surrounding rooftops. They found themselves struck down by the

Child's Celestial Father, or indeed Kaila, who acted as Sebastien's shadow and made sure that the Child came and went in secret.

Throughout all this, Sebastien was marvellous. Those who I allowed to speak with him, even for a short time, came out transfigured. To hear them tell it, the Child sensed worries they'd been too shy to confide, and told them things they had not known about themselves. Sebastien disliked mediating in disputes, so I discouraged people who sought that kind of help. We didn't want the city magistrates on our backs just yet. At least, not until we had enough of a following amongst people with power to cushion the impact.

'The line of business we're in, trouble is bound to find us sooner or later,' Kaila warned me, 'so best keep a bag at the door ready for a quick escape.'

*

Of course, Sebastien's wisdom was partially a product of Folkhert's joyful hospitality in the evenings. 'Come for a bite to eat,' he'd say, or, 'Step round for something to drink. And I don't mean barley water.' The old man seemed to be spinning quite a social web, with himself as the garrulous spider in the middle. I made sure to be there too, and listened closely when he would sidle up to me, cup in hand, and whisper: 'Now, I've been told this in the strictest confidence, and you must promise not to tell a soul.' I made a promise to myself never to tell him any of my secrets.

Sebastien understood people uncommonly well and had a knack for drawing out information without them noticing. I felt sad that he couldn't find a better use for his talents than this day-to-day existence of thievery and deceit.

'It's easy,' he explained. 'Everyone has a big worry. That's a given. It doesn't even matter if it's something small that bothers them; when they stand in front of me it's a big worry. Often it's about love or money. It makes a difference whether they're a man or a woman, and how old they are, all sorts of things. A poor young woman comes to me: Chances are she wants to marry but doesn't have the money for a dowry. When they're a bit older, I might guess something like, 'You're worried for your child, aren't you?' and you'll see their lower lip quivering, their eyes moisten. Every decent mother is worried about her child in some way. Now, take a middle-aged man, well-to-do. I look at his finger, see a wedding band. 'Your wife,' I say, and shake my head in sorrow, 'if only she wouldn't stand in the way.' And if I see that look in his face, I know he plans to squander his money on some luxury, or a mistress. I don't even need to know what it is. So, I tell him to be prudent and send him back to his wife.'

'What about me? Would I be so easy to read?' I asked. I was disappointed at humanity being reducible to so few wants, all individuality lost as he pushed them this way and that. It was too calculated for me. But Sebastien was on a roll now – the nature of his craft was such that he could only boast of it to us, and Kaila had heard it all before.

'Alright, so it's not always that easy. These are gene-
ralities, which I make seem like big revelations. I can ask
questions which don't look important, but lead me to other
information. I make vague statements, give a sketched
outline, and let them tell me what it means.'

He grabbed my arms with both his hands and looked
me at me with wide open eyes. 'Ymke, I see a huge figure
in your life. A man. He's lost to you.'

'Yes, I see,' I said.

'Easy as that. It might be your father, it might be a
former lover, maybe a brother killed in a war. Usually,
they'll tell me who it is.'

'I'm sure they do. They're confiding in Kristjoffel the
Child though, not in Sebastien the Scoundrel.'

People who'd known Kristjoffel as a child were
trickier. Most people who had been close to him had been
killed alongside him, or left the city during the Great Purge
that followed. In the weeks that followed the Child's
Return, several survivors of his youth came straggling
back. Sebastien looked closely at Folkhert's reactions to
them in deciding how to play each one of them, invariably
aided by the old man's fondness for reminiscence. The
passage of time helped enormously, and if they did have
their doubts, they were eager to close their eyes and join
the old friends at the table. We worried that when these
old friends started to turn up they'd want to gather about
him as they'd done in the old days, becoming permanent
fixtures of the household, but we need not have feared.
Most were pulled away by the lives they'd built up after
their previous one had gone up in flames alongside the

Child and, as for the few who were reluctant to leave, the Child reminded them that they had not been there in his greatest hour of need, and that they had no claim on him. Father Folkhert showed just enough disappointment to be polite as they packed their bags, but had trouble disguising his relief when they left. He clearly enjoyed being the only one from the old days to remain at the boy's side.

*

Of course, not everyone was as easily swayed or bought, and there were plenty who didn't believe in the Return of the Child. I would have worried if there weren't. Most of them just shrugged, shook their heads and went on with their lives. There were some, though, who actively denounced Kristjoffel. It takes a certain kind of person to do that: Someone else has something they lack, even something intangible like joy or peace of mind, and they have to shout about it or even try to destroy it.

These unwelcome characters invariably met with an ill turn in their fortunes. Not all of it was our doing either, as those who did believe, or wanted to believe, stopped frequenting their shops and turned away when they met them in the street. We took an active role if these gnats were particularly bothersome, and what we cooked up for them was more elaborate. We had the greatest fun thinking up increasingly bizarre plots. Several of them involved horse manure: It might fall on people out of nowhere, be delivered in wagonloads to their front doors, or find its way into their food. Everyone loves manure, so long as it's someone else falling in it. Whenever this happened, soon everyone knew about it. And they could point and say, 'It's his own fault. He doesn't believe the Child has Returned.'

*

Though we shared a house, the three of us didn't see much of each other. Sebastien flitted in and out, either as the Child or performing the Child's miracles in secret. He still slept under the table whenever he could, sometimes with Kaila and I having breakfast right over his head. We discussed what the day would bring, and then I'd go to Father Folkhert, and Kaila went out to bestow either curses or miracles upon people. There was the Miracle of the Drunkard's Wife, for example. A washerwoman had cried in Sebastien's arms about her husband, who drank away all her profits and left her no money to feed the children. The Child magically turned all the wine in the house into water. It's easy enough to do if you can break in and swap a few casks around. Of course, the husband flew into a rage, but then the Child appeared at the window and promised him a worse fate if he didn't mend his ways. A mirror and a shielded lamp gave Sebastien a most uncanny glow in the dusk, and when I met the washerwoman the following week, she said that her husband hadn't touched a drop since and had even found himself a job.

There were reverse burglaries, with Kaila and Sebastien secretly distributing some of the Child's growing wealth: The courtesan fallen on hard times found a purse of money and the deeds to a small shop; the wheelwright whose hands had grown arthritic got coins too, but also a jar of salve and the address of a skilled wise woman; and the old folk of the neighbourhood were provided for too. The gifts were always wrapped in a cheap woodcut print of the Child, so people knew who they had come from.

Then there were miracles that were attributed to the Child, but were not our doing. Belief can be a strong force in itself, we learned. But we also got a glimpse of things to come when two old women claimed an early sighting of the Child. One of them had lost her purse in the market, and the Child, though he had not made himself known as such at the time, had returned it to her.

One night Kaila came back from her miracle rounds early. She slipped into bed carefully, but was soon tossing and turning enough to keep me awake. I asked what was bothering her.

'How long do we keep this up? It started as a way for us to make money, and for you to get even about your book, but it's all getting out of hand. They're already giving the Child credit for good things we didn't do. What if he starts getting blamed for really big misfortunes? What if some non-believer dies suspiciously?'

I looked into the blackness of her eyes, but I couldn't read her expression in the faint light that comes before dawn. I reached out a hand and laid it on her cheek. She tried to smile, but then remembered something: 'And Sebastien, have you noticed that he's not quite himself?'

It was true. Sebastien had grown quieter and more serious over the past few weeks. I hadn't heard him laugh lately about the people he'd seen during the day, or brag of his skills in deceiving them. No longer satisfied with telling them things he shouldn't know, he was trying to help everyone who crossed his path. He seemed to have developed a conscience.

'He's changed, but not for the worst. Maybe he's grown up a bit. But you're right, he can't play the Child forever. The more people want him, the harder it'll be.'

'I suppose the Child could tell the people to carry on the good work in his name, and just leave. Although...' she sighed. 'That means Sebastien and I really will have to leave.'

'I know,' I said, and pulled her close, 'But we'll end on a high note.'

*

We were still awake when morning sun and birdsong filtered through the oak shutters. Both of us were reluctant to leave the comfort of the bed and each other, and we were still mulling over our decision.

'I know what we'll do. How about that woman whose husband has a wandering eye and loose fists?' Kaila said, from behind my back. I rolled over.

'Yes, it's got to be her. I noticed the bruises on her face, though she kept the hood of her cloak up, even in this heat. She hardly dared to speak and she flinched when I touched her. I asked her name, and she gave not her own but her husband's.'

I whispered, as the woman had done: "'Eisenschau. Sigir Eisenschau's wife." So, what do you have in mind?'

Kaila told me, and the bed trembled with our laughter.

*

Sebastien took the news of the Child's imminent disappearance well. Until he'd met Kaila, life had been a series of wagons he'd hitched rides on, and whenever a wagon stopped, he hopped onto another. Kaila seemed relieved too, and was full of energy as she began preparing our final caper. She was louder than usual, though, and she laughed a bit too quickly. I tried not to think too deeply about how I'd pick up my life again when they'd gone – when *she'd* gone – as I didn't want to spoil our last days together with sadness. I reckoned that maybe I wouldn't go back to being just a scribe. I could stay involved with Father Folkhert and the Child's work. Let something good and lasting grow from our deception. Other than that, I pushed away all thoughts of the future.

*

I'd made a visit to a local wise woman I knew through Father Folkhert, and returned with a small vial, carefully wrapped in a black cloth. When we'd told her, more or less, what it was for, she'd chuckled and given it to us with her blessing. She was not one of the Child's followers, yet she and Father Folkhert got along well.

'She tends the body, as I tend the soul, and both of us are travellers off the beaten path,' he'd explained. That's what I liked about the old man: He wasn't dogmatic about the people he was prepared to consort with. And after all, he gave me a lot of his time, and had been good to me in his way.

Kaila showed me the costume she'd created, and which she'd be wearing that night.

'Trust me; I've worked disguises like this before, and to great effect,' she promised, when I chuckled at the collection of fabrics, lumps and feathers. 'Also, this is for you. It's unmade rather than made, and I'm sure you'll look great in it.'

I looked at the dress she held up. The hems were ragged where it had been shortened. 'Look at the state of it! And how's it going to cover me?'

'It's not supposed to. At least, not all of you.'

It was a hot summer's evening, and never had I been more grateful for one. My dress didn't give me much warmth, and although I was having a bad day with my leg, I left my walking stick behind, because the kind of man we were setting a trap for would be put off by it. My hair was unbraided and Kaila had made up my face, and shown me the result. I didn't recognise the woman in the mirror.

'Men love that stuff,' she'd said, and Sebastien's face confirmed this. We'd sent him away.

When Sigir Eisenschau came around the corner on his way to the inn, I was waiting for him. He was small and wiry, and had more hair on his knuckles than his head. His was the rolling walk of someone used to settling arguments with his fists rather than with words. I fluttered my eyelashes, thrust my chest at him and asked, with a wriggle of my hips, where he was going. Not for one moment did I believe that any of this looked natural. It didn't matter to Eisenschau.

'To the pub, love. Fancy one yourself?'

'No, I can't,' I said, making a sigh of the last word, and sticking out my lower lip. 'I moved in today, just around the corner, but somehow I can't get the door open. I'm looking for a strong man who can help me jiggle the key in the lock.'

Forestalling any more flirtation, he took my arm and paraded us off in the direction I gave him. The door, of course, was unlocked, and the wooden prop with which we'd made it stick gave way quickly enough. Still, he was very proud of himself. I stood in the small hallway and glanced up the wooden stairs.

'I'm ever so grateful; I don't know what I'd have done without you. I'd offer you a drink, but I'm sure that you'll have a wife to go home to?'

'Off to the Wheelies,' he said. We'd made sure of that; she'd been collected and brought to Sebastien for a special blessing. Eisenschau hopped up the stairs without further invitation. The rooms upstairs were the sort you could rent by the week, day or even hour. Kaila had rented one for the whole night, but I expected to be gone long before the morning. I knew Kaila would make sure of that.

*

The room was sparsely furnished. Aside from the bed there was just a stool in the corner, and a small table holding some bottles and glasses. A decorative frieze of stylised flowers ran along the whitewashed wall, while the ceiling, between the heavy beams, was a riot of painted satyrs and nymphs. You see that sometimes: the Otasringar sense of order can abide only the simplest decorations in the line of sight, but the human desire for colour and frippery has to come out somewhere. Here, it had exploded onto the ceilings.

Eisenschau plonked down on the bed, while I made him the promised drink. I felt his gaze on my backside and clenched my teeth. I took a deep breath and turned round again. He already had his shoes and shirt off. He tried to grab me and I swung out of the way quicker than I'd thought possible with my bad leg.

'Not so fast,' I said, wagging a finger and smiling. 'We've got all the time in the world. Here, drink this and I'll make myself another. Help us both relax and enjoy ourselves.'

I took as long as I could in making my own drink and stirring it. I made quite a show of uncorking a new bottle of wine and wiping the bottle's neck dry with a cloth. Sigir Eisenschau sat slumped backwards on the bed, with a big grin on his face, and his eyes slowly closing. The sleeping draught had worked exactly as the wise woman had predicted.

I sat for a while on the far edge of the bed, and watched a fly land on his forehead. It wandered down his nose and still he did not stir. It was enough. The wise woman had warned us that the sleeping draught was quick to work, but also quick to wear off, so I didn't wait any longer. I retrieved a dark cloak from under the bed, not the one I'd got from Father Folkhert, but one of my own, and hastened down the stairs. I opened the door to the street and whistled. Kaila slipped inside with a bag slung over her shoulder.

I placed a lamp on either side of the bed while she got ready, one covered with a green scarf, the other in red. Then I crouched in the corner of the dingy room, my cloak wrapped around me. Kaila crept onto the bed and positioned herself over Eisenschau.

'His breathing is changing. He's coming out of it,' she whispered. One side of her face was lit bright red, the other sickly green, with pools of shadow for eyes. She grinned at me, baring carved wooden fangs.

She lifted one foot, placed it on his chest, then stepped on with the other. With a final snort, Eisenschau woke up and opened his eyes. The sound started in the back of his throat, a deep moan that held on, then loosed as a wail from the wide 'O' of his mouth.

The demon on his chest bent towards him, its eyes bulging, and blew stinking breath into his face. It spread its stubby wings and planted a paw with long, sharp nails on his forehead. Then Kaila growled the words I'd written for her: 'I am the ghost of each time you hit your wife, the spectre of each harsh and cruel word. I am the beast born from your lust and violence. Sigir Eisenschau, I've come for you!'

Eisenschau's legs started to spasm, then kick, and as Kaila leapt free, he scrambled backwards against the headboard. I leapt from my corner and spread out my cape. I'd sewn white triangles into its red lining, creating the effect of a giant mouth ready to devour him.

'Repent!' I shrieked at him, and bared my fangs.

'I'll never hurt her again. Never look at another woman. I, I...' He sprang up, and went howling down the stairs, almost taking the door with him.

Kaila and I fell down laughing on the bed.

*

We hadn't been sure whether to inform Father Folkhert of the Child's departure, but decided it was only fair. The old man was not at all surprised when I told him, though he was still heartbroken.

'I was blessed to be reunited with the Child, but I knew that as I left him so long ago to join my family, so he must leave me. These weeks have been such a gift to me that an old man could not hope for more. And I did so enjoy our little chats. Ymke, my dear, do you still have the cloak I gave you? I would share a last meal with you and the Child, and I think the Child should wear it.' He hesitated. It was obvious to me that something was weighing on his mind. 'I have news to impart. I had meant to save it, but seeing that the Child, well... this evening, then?'

A gloomy silence hung in my kitchen until, mid-afternoon, Kaila rose.

'Right. Enough of this. We need a drink.' She produced a bottle of tolerable wine and poured us each a goblet. We sat down with the memories of the past few weeks, and soon Kaila stood hunched on the table to give Sebastien an impression of the bird-demon creature she'd been.

'And there he went, half naked, screaming through the streets, and I almost flew after him with my little stubby wings.'

'I'm glad you didn't, as I'd have had to go after you. With that dress I was in, I'm not sure who'd be in more trouble: Eisenschau, you or myself!'

'He's not been home since, and word has gone round that he's followed a wandering band of Brothers out of town, wearing sackcloth on his back and a wheel around his neck. His wife's still waiting for him, worried out of her mind. But she'll get over him.'

Kaila looked out of the window, and saw the length of the shadows on the buildings opposite. 'We should go,' she said. Sebastien nodded and picked up the folded cloak that Father Folkhert had given me.

Kaila went ahead of us and quickly disappeared between the buildings. Sebastien and I walked slowly and in silence until we were a few streets removed from the square, me in my old cloak and he in the simple robes of a lay Brother, hunched over and with the hood pulled down. On the corner before Grauwalt Alley spilt out onto Guderia's Mile, he glanced round, saw that nobody was near, and removed Father Folkhert's cloak from inside his robes and put it on. Then he climbed the fence and used wall anchors and ledges to scramble up the building. He waved at me from its flat roof, then disappeared.

On the square I found myself unable to make it through the crowds. I was spotted by one of the Alabaster Brothers, who cleared a path for me to Folkhert's door, and there Brother Walther let me in. It didn't take long before Sebastien also joined us, having travelled over the roofs of the neighbouring buildings.

Conversation during dinner died and was resurrected, with effort, several times. Sebastien smiled wanly as Father Folkhert ladled him a third bowl of soup.

'You're too thin, my boy, much too thin. You've got to eat well, you've got a long journey ahead of you.' The old man was stalling, I thought. I put down my spoon.

'Father Folkhert, you had some news for the Child?'

'Yes, yes. They're going to demolish my home.' He raised his hands. 'I know what you'll want to say, but I won't hear of it. I've had a good time here, and now the Child is leaving it just won't be the same. They've also bought the houses of the neighbours.'

'Who are 'they'?' I asked.

'The Brothers, of course.' He reached behind him and produced a roll of paper. 'Here, Ymke, help me with this.'

Unrolled, it showed images of what the square would look like, and the cathedral that was to loom over it. Part of the square would be taken over by a staircase of about twenty paces wide, with steps high enough that climbing it would have anyone on their knees. The stairs led to the sole tower, on the left side of the cathedral. The cathedral entrance was a gaping maw, a huge semi-circle surrounded by a heavy, decorated arch. This portal sat in the middle of the tower and was almost squashed by the window above it. It was the one window of significance, in the shape of a huge, four-spoked Wheel.

It was monstrous. I saw that it would consume not only Father Folkhert's house and those of his immediate neighbours, but all the other houses that looked out over the square. In their place, a high wall would surround the cathedral, studded with squat towers and punctured with small windows, made to look out on an otherwise empty square. I thought of the baker, Goodwife Kunelore, even the man from the junkshop – all the people of Guderian Square who I'd come to regard as my own people. Father Folkhert mistook my expression for awe.

'It's beautiful, isn't it? The cathedral they will build here to His glory,' he nodded at Sebastien, 'will be here for all the people, and will stand long after my death. They say I may be buried in it. Brother Walther told me last night, and I wanted to be the one to tell you the good news. Ah, that'll be him!'

We heard the front door being thrown open. Sebastien and I jumped, but Folkhert shuffled to the hall, a smile on his face. We heard voices: Father Folkhert's, Brother Walther's, and others that I recognised as the harsh, excitable voices of other Alabaster Brothers.

'Something's wrong,' I whispered to Sebastien, but there was no time to react. Walther barrelled in, flanked by several companions who looked just as pious. They were wearing their full regalia, complete with pointed hoods that spilled over their white robes and left only their faces bare, and heavy chains, weighted further with medals and interlinked plaques.

'Soup?' said Sebastien, gamely holding up the ladle. They strode towards him and seized him before he could put the thing down. The soup went flying. Father Folkhert shot me an apologetic look as I was shoved aside. He squeezed his hands to nervous fists and shuffled over to Sebastien, who was held down on the ground by two of the Brothers. He struggled to his knees and buried his face in the folds of the Child's robes. Then Sebastien was dragged from the room, his legs kicking fruitlessly in the air.

'Lemme go! I'm not Kristjoffel,' Sebastien shouted. 'I'm Sebastien, an innocent thief!' The stream of un-Childlike language that issued from the hall was abruptly cut off.

'Yes, yes,' said Folkhert. 'How well I remember our playing that game in the old days! Never mind that now; the Wheel has turned. You can go home, Child, and this time I will be here to witness it.'

'What's going on here?' I demanded finally. I cursed myself; I might have slipped away, instead of just sitting there and then opening my big mouth and drawing attention to myself.

Walther turned to me, not disguising his disgust. 'Of course, you're here to interfere, but you'll interfere no more. The Brotherhood has discussed matters, and we believe the faith has been reinvigorated enough. The Child has given the people his blessings, and even miracles. What else is left for him to give?'

'Father Folkhert? Don't you realise what they are going to do?'

'Yes, dear, and it will be glorious!'

I struggled up from my chair, and stumbled through the hall. My way was blocked by two Brothers. Over their shoulders I saw Sebastien in his white robes and the ancient cloak, still held by the Brothers, though a hastily tied gag had come undone, and he was shouting something. His words were drowned out by the noise of the crowd that had gathered. They chanted in unison:

'Turn the Wheel! Turn the Wheel!'

Wheels fastened to sticks were thrust above the crowd, turning in the summer breeze.

I caught a glimpse of the washerwoman, and the courtesan. They were cheering for the Child, as were the wheelwright and so many others he had helped. I tried to force my way past the Brothers, who'd turned to watch the spectacle, but I might as well have been an insect for all the good it did. One of them reached behind him and shoved me off.

Sigir Eisenschau! He hadn't left town after all, but he had joined the Brotherhood. Maybe not so strange; on reflection, Eisenschau and Brother Walther were cut from the same damnable cloth. My eye fell on the walking stick I'd left in the hall earlier. I grabbed it, swung it with all the strength I had at Eisenschau and lunged past him as he fell to his knees.

I stumbled towards the spectators and hoped to disappear amongst them, but knew I wasn't fast enough. I felt the other Brother behind me. A shape darted from the crowd, grabbed my wrist and pulled me in. Kaila. Flashes of metal, shrieks and people giving way, then she was back at my side. She slung an arm around my waist and shouldered us away. 'Coming through,' she shouted, 'Make way! Lady's with child!' I kept stumbling over my long dress, but Kaila kept me upright and dragged me onwards.

We caught our breath behind a market stall abandoned by its owner. Children had climbed on top of it and craned their necks over the crowds, trampling the wooden plaques, the cheap earthenware and paper flags, all with the image of the Child. A big cheer went up from the crowd. Kaila screamed at me what I already knew.

'They're going to Wheel him! They're going to Wheel Sebastien!'

I clambered onto the wooden stand. Kaila gave me a push when I had trouble getting my leg up.

'What do you see?'

'They've brought out a Wheel on a cart!' It was a simple farmer's wagon, big and solid, which had been white-washed and decorated with flowers. The Wheel it carried was big, taller than a man, made of wood and with the four spokes I'd seen in so many representations. Two draught horses waited patiently as one of the Brothers addressed the crowd. I'd met him before, a boring man with a never-ending supply of words stored behind a flat slab of a face, and a mouth like a crack. I couldn't hear what he was saying, and I don't think anyone but the people closest to him could. Sebastien struggled and shrieked behind him. He was a prop in his own play now, no longer the main actor.

'Burn the Wheel! Burn the Wheel!' The crowd now chanted, not listening to the screams of their beloved

Child. I slid off the stand, Kaila catching me.

'If we can take the cart, we can get away,' I said.

'It's risky.' She looked at me, trying to guess how much I was prepared for. She needn't have worried.

'It's that, or watch Sebastien burn.'

'Come on, then,' she said. We made our way through the crowd again, now returning to the front rows. Once again I leaned heavily on Kaila, while I explained what I had in mind. It wasn't much of a plan, but it was all we had. Near the edge of the crowd we stopped. She thrust a dagger into my belt. It left a red smear on the white of my dress. She threw her arms around me and I bent forward, burying my face in her dark hair. Just a second, then I let her go.

'Be careful. See you in a bit.' She raised a quick hand, then disappeared. I hitched up my hood, straightened my back, and slipped through the last bands of people that separated me from Sebastien and that dreadful Wheel.

The Brothers spotted me immediately, as I'd expected. My first priority was to prevent them taking out their comrades' injuries on me. Had Kaila killed them? I didn't know. Three of them marched up and seemed ready to pummel me. I held up a hand, as if that could stop them, and gave them my sternest look.

'Take me to Brother Walther,' I said. Their fists stopped in the air. While they looked at each other for a suitable reaction, I walked past them, careful not to drag my leg. They let me pass, then followed.

On the wagon, Sebastien's wrists had already been lashed to the Wheel. Two Brothers held his legs, one each, and a third worked on his ankles with a rope.

The Alabaster Brother with the flat face droned on, looking daggers at me as I passed him. One of the Brothers gave me a push and I landed right in the arms of Brother Sigir Eisenschau. Quickly, I was dragged out of sight, behind the wagon. He had me pinned against him, my back to his chest

'Thought I wouldn't recognise you, did you? Clever trick you played on me. Bet you had a good laugh. But guess who'll be laughing next.' Flecks of his spit flew into my ear.

'That won't be...' I tried, but I was out of breath. His boots were sturdy, and no matter how I stamped on his feet and kicked at his shins, he did not let me go, and my hands were unable to break his arm away from my throat. He squeezed and I choked. The other Brothers turned away, back to the real spectacle. Above me, Sebastien screamed, but nobody listened. Black flowers erupted in my vision.

'Wait,' I heard. 'Let her speak.' Father Folkhert. His face emerged through the blackness. Sigir Eisenschau released his arm a little. It was all I needed.

'I want to die with the Child,' I said, between gasps and coughs.

Brother Sigir's arm remained around my throat while he thought it over, then he let me go. I fell on the ground, heard the clatter of metal. My dagger. Under the wagon, out of my reach. I could lunge for it, stab him. But even if I killed him, what then? No. I looked up.

'Please. Let me die with the Child.'

Father Folkhert stooped and stretched out his thin arm. 'I am proud of you, Ymke. Nothing pleases me more than to die with the Child, knowing that you too will be at my side.'

'Father Folkhert. You can't!'

'Yes, I can. It's what I want. Once I deserted the Child. Not again. My bones, our bones, shall be the mortar with which the Child's cathedral will be built.' He smiled, his eyes moist slits. Sigir Eisenschau appeared beside him and shrugged.

'Very well then. Both of you burn. But let's be quick about it.' He tied my hands behind my back with a length of rope and pushed me up the ladder. Father Folkhert waved away his help and followed me up onto the wagon. Sebastien was still screaming, his hands and feet tied to the four spokes of the Wheel. Eisenschau's strong hand pushed me down into the straw, then he jumped off, leaving just one Brother with us, who held a lit torch and was chatting with his colleagues on the ground. When he glanced our way I saw that it was Brother Walther. Of course.

Father Folkhert waved at the crowds, and laughed as they cheered him on and raised their stick-Wheels in salute. Then he sat down next to me, helped me sit upright and brushed the straw off me with his hand.

'Worry not, girl. There's a Child in all of us. You, me, the good people there. And while some of us die, others may live to spread his glory.'

I shook my head, felt tears coming. The old man grabbed my shoulder, fixed his eyes on me.

'No, Ymke. Pay attention. It is happening.'

I looked to my other side, where Brother Walther reached his free hand up the Wheel to one of the studs that lined the rim. He grunted as he pulled. Sebastien shrieked. The crowd went wild.

'The Wheel turns! The Wheel turns!'

Brother Walther raised the torch and pumped his fist as they chanted. Between my wrists I felt the cold metal of a blade. Father Folkhert hushed me and worked at the rope until it fell away.

'Not yet. Wait.'

With a quick flick of his arm Brother Walther gave the Wheel more speed. Sebastien was quiet now, though his mouth, when it flashed by, was still wide open. Once more, Brother Walther raised his torch, basking in the screams of the crowd, then lowered it. He stepped back, and I saw fingers of fire spread through the straw.

'Not yet.'

Father Folkhert rose and waved both his hands at the crowd. He then turned towards the flames and took a deep breath. Brother Walther stepped aside to let him pass. The old man smiled at him and moved a sandalled foot towards the flames. Then he planted his foot down and threw himself against Brother Walther with all the strength in his wiry frame, so that both of them disappeared over the wagon's side.

I scrambled to the front of the wagon and grabbed the horse's reins from the seat.

'Pull!' I screamed, and whipped the reins. The horses set off at a trot. People moved or were pushed aside. Their hands reached out to the wagon - whether to touch it or to stop it, I don't know. Sebastien started screaming again and I looked round to see that flames were licking at the Wheel's posts.

'Pull! Stupid beasts, what's wrong with you!' Any other horses would have run from the fire. These had been bred into plodding docility. I sat properly on the bench now. A shrill whistle sounded ahead of me. Kaila. I searched the crowd.

'Ymke!'

She waved at me from the Guderian Arch. She hung above the crowd, perched with both feet on a small ridge in the masonry, holding onto the plump helmet of one of Guderia's fair soldiers with one hand. I held the horses in slightly as I steered them through the arch, and the thud behind me told me she'd landed. Waves of shouting rolled behind us.

'You alright?'

'Aye. Give me your cloak. Quick.'

I fumbled with the catch, then shook the cloak off my shoulders. I steered the horses around a corner, onto Guderia's Mile. I bent forward and slapped them on the backside. They tossed their heads, eyes rolling and teeth champing, but did not pick up their pace. I cursed them. Dray horses, good for nothing but a steady trot.

I darted quick glances behind me, saw Kaila kicking away burning straw and beating at the flames with my cloak. She threw her body against the Wheel until it stopped spinning. Sword in hand, she hacked at Sebastien's bonds, quickly freeing him. He clambered onto the bench next to me, violently coughing and retching. He'd be fine.

From the sides of the road people shouted and pointed, running away from us or towards us. Behind us the mob still followed, shouting and waving their stick-Wheels. Some of them threw their sticks at us like spears, but they clattered on the cobbles far behind us.

'Dung and piss!' Kaila crashed backwards against the bench. Waves of heat beat my back.

Her face blackened and sweaty, Kaila's eyes were wild as they found mine. 'Need your help.' She darted away again.

I thrust the reins at Sebastien, who still sat bent over, and turned round. Kaila was again beating at the flames, my cloak a ragged, smouldering mess. She'd managed to beat the fire away from the front of the wagon, but there was no hope of extinguishing the Wheel. The wood must have been prepared, the way the flames leapt and roared. I thought of Sebastien tied on the Wheel and a wave of revulsion hit me.

'Guard me,' Kaila said, and threw me the smouldering cape. She slid down on the rough wood of the wagon, her knees drawn up, feet braced against the Wheel. I beat the flames away from her as best as I could, but saw the sparks that landed on her, saw the hot wood that singed her flesh.

She let out a cry. Her nails dug into the smoking boards of the wagon as she stretched every muscle in her back, in her legs. The Wheel rocked away from her, then halted, then slowly, slowly its wooden support beams gave way. Then it fell away from us, crashed through the wagon's back, and bounced on the street behind us. We looked at

that great burning Wheel, ploughing into its worshippers, then set to work again until everything that burned was either kicked off the wagon or smothered.

We collapsed in a heap, singed and sore, but alive. We both started laughing wildly, and each time one of us came out of it, gasping for breath, one look at the other had us back in tears.

'It's nice that you ladies are having fun back there,' Sebastien said eventually, 'but can you tell me how to make these stubborn beasts stop?'

*

We would no longer be safe in the city; that was immediately clear to us. Kaila and Sebastien were fairly unconcerned about this, used as they were to leaving places in a hurry. But I had a life here that had suddenly gone up in flames, and looked to Kaila to help me through it.

'So, what do we do?'

'We abandon the wagon and take the horses. We go home, pack up and leave. We've got our escape bags already, and you've got between here and there to think about what else you want to bring. We travel light.'

I wandered through my house with my mind's eye, past the shelves and cupboards. In the end it was not that difficult, and I left with little more than I had arrived with a few years earlier. We steered our horses past neighbours who headed towards the commotion in the distance, and we were long gone by the time any mob would reach my home.

That night we camped underneath the giant trees of Otaswalt, built a fire and took stock. Aside from some small cuts, burns and bruises I was fine. Kaila had seen me flinching when I came off the horse.

'Your leg, how bad is it?' she asked.

'I'll not be walking much for the next few days,' I answered. She sent Sebastien for more firewood, then told me to hitch up my dress and lie on my belly. She sat down on her knees beside me. At first her hands were comfortable on my thigh, hip and lower back, but later she massaged the muscles with more force. It was hard work, even for her, and I winced when she seemed to have reached the bone itself. She hushed me.

'Another thing I picked up in the army. It'll be worth it. '

Kaila herself had suffered quite a few burns, but none of them were really serious. I was surprised to find a cut across her arm. 'Those Brothers had knives too. Shouldn't have pulled them though,' she said, and shrugged. If the burns or that cut left any marks, they would only add to the landscape of her scars.

Despite having been strapped to the Wheel itself, Sebastien came out of this ordeal the best of we three. His hair was singed and his eyebrows never grew back quite right, but rotating above the fire meant that he was never close to the flames long enough to really get hurt. He couldn't stop reminding Kaila, though, that their schemes always ended up on stages of sorts, and that the smell of freshly carpented wood made him break out in a sweat. Clearly they had stories that they hadn't told me, just as I kept my secrets.

It was ironic, too, that the moth-eaten cloak had protected his back from the flames once they'd crept up the Wheel's supports. I wondered how much foresight Father Folkhert really had, and what he knew, or feared, when he asked Sebastien to wear it.

*

Speaking of Folkhert, I wrote to thank him. Of course, I waited a while, and had to use various go-betweens to deliver my letter, but he received it in the end. I was surprised to receive a missive from him in return.

'Hail to my wayward Sister from her elderly Brother,' he wrote. 'All is well with me; I am content on the bench in front of my little house. When winter came, the crowds left, but in spring it remains quiet on the square. Except for the people who live here, that is, and the birds who sing above me in the pear tree. I feed them each day. I'll have to clean their mess myself now, because Brother Walther has gone. Or maybe I'll leave it. It doesn't harm me. They've made a nest, and I hope I'll still be here when the nestlings fly. There won't be any cathedral, but the Child is alive in me and in the people.'

He signed the letter with a small, four-spoked wheel. He'd scribbled something underneath, against the very edge of the page.

'It was very naughty what you and your friends did, but I forgive you. That too is the way of the Child.'

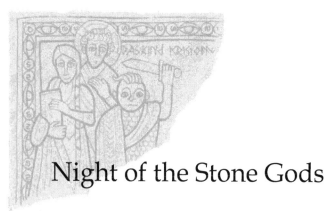

Night of the Stone Gods

They had travelled all day. Autumn had set the leaves ablaze, and even though the sun had not yet set, there was no warmth to be had in these woods. The acrid smell of damp earth clung to them and pulled at them, and the mushrooms and berries they'd foraged were the season's only concessions to their survival. Ocke knew that his bride could not go on for much longer, and not just because of the growing cold. He scanned the trail and peered through the trees for any hint of habitation; a door to knock on, to ask for hospitality, if only for a single night's good sleep. Surely it would be safe, and they were now beyond the reach of her father's men? Surely nobody would send them away? Surely - Deep in thought, he did not notice that Addyerth no longer rode beside him.

'Ocke!' she called, and he turned just in time to see her slide off her horse. She stumbled to a tree and leaned against it. He urged his horse towards her.

'Addyerth, we can't -' he started, then saw the tears in her eyes, and the way she clutched the fabric of her travel-stained dress, her knuckles white. This was not how it was supposed to be. He sighed. 'Very well, then.'

The height of the trees and the thickness of the shrubs had hidden the true nature of the place as they approached it. If she hadn't spotted the narrow, almost overgrown pathway that led inward, they would have skirted the copse altogether. But she had seen the path, and they had walked their unwilling horses down it, and now they stood in the clearing. It was a quiet place; the silence was not the absence of sound, but the hush of a breath held in and slowly released. He did not trust it.

'A superstition, nothing more,' Addyerth said, a little too fast: 'The sky is so clear; we can sleep right here in the open.' He knew how tired she was of curling up under trees, amongst the creatures that sheltered and scuttled there.

He turned slowly, taking in the dozen stones, each twice the height of a tall man, that stood in a wide circle around them. 'I know you find it foolish,' he said, 'But my ancestors knew places like this. Their names wore away with time, but the warning was passed down: 'Never sleep where the stone gods watch.' I've known that since I was a child.'

'Then let them watch over us,' she said, and she unbuckled the blanket roll from the pack. 'If this place has any power at all, then it must be protective. I barely spotted the path; no-one will know we're here. Just one night.'

He shook his head, but the cold and the fading light and the ache in his muscles overruled him.

Indeed, they watched that night, with their cold, un-blinking eyes carved into stern, rudimentary faces by some stoneworker of old. As he waited for sleep, he wondered who they were, these forgotten gods, and who had worshipped them – and how. Had these stone faces looked on as cattle were sacrificed in their midst, where his wife now slept? Humans, even? He shuddered, and looked at Addyerth's still form and sighed. The ghost of the hopelessness he had felt, that last day in the palace, clutched at his heart.

*

The corridors that led through the Markgraf's palace had seemed never-ending, and he had to resist hurrying through them. He'd only been there at nighttime before, and only in the unguarded and little used passages. At the vast door inlaid with gold and ivory, the chamberlain told him to wait, then slipped inside.

Knowing he would be given very little time, he'd rehearsed different things to say, depending on how he was received.

'My lord, if your daughter's happiness means anything to you, then let us wed,' he might say, or: 'My lord, you are a just man. What better justice than to grant a man and woman in love the licence to marry?' He'd wondered whether he should square his shoulders and plant his feet, and demand the hand of the woman he loved, as if it were a right that would not be refused, or whether it would be wiser to throw himself on his lord's mercy instead.

He'd examined his appearance again. His shoes were still clean, his new breeches smart, and it was a moment's work to straighten his coat and remove a little lint. Then the door had opened again, and he was announced. He'd walked up to the dais where his lord loomed above him. He'd bowed deeply, as was the custom.

'My lord,' he'd begun. A raised hand cut him off and steel grey eyes peered at him. Then his lord had spoken.

'Would that be a merchant's coat you are wearing?'

His courage had shrivelled up, along with any hope that he would be allowed to marry the woman he loved.

They'd turned to their gods for help, but no matter how much they prayed and pleaded, the gods remained silent. So they had married in secret and disappeared. Should he now pray to these stone gods for their blessing? How could these gods guard their journey if he didn't know their names, and if he himself didn't know where they were going?

*

He sat pondering until long after their fire had died, and the gods were nothing more than black shadows against the night sky. He eventually fell asleep to the gentle sound of the horses snorting and grazing, then woke again with the first birds. He let Addyerth sleep while he packed their few things. She was so tired these days, unused to the outdoor life, to spending the best part of the day on horseback. The elder gods were still there. They looked so different in the morning light. Whether that was good or bad, he had no way of knowing. But it was warmer today, he felt it already, and that at least was something.

Then it was time to go. Gently, he shook her awake.

'I dreamed about them,' she said, 'Or maybe they visited me in my dream. They told me of the little girl we'll have.'

She smiled, and her hand rested on her belly. 'She'll be kind and courageous, and see a great many places and do extraordinary things.'

The Forbidden Room

Quite how she found that space, she didn't remember afterwards. A child's curiosity, coupled with boredom and loneliness, and maybe an instinct, just a feeling at the back of the mind that the walls didn't quite meet, a hint of a draught, dust disturbed by a leaning hand, or a wooden wall sounding hollow… interest was sparked, and the girl gave it all the scrutiny she could muster with a mind that did not have to worry about anything else. She found a hidden catch, and a panel in the back of the cupboard bed sprang open.

When her father came back from the fields and walked into the kitchen, Ymke's smile froze. She'd never had cause to fear her father before, yet never had she seen his face look like that. His mouth was like an upside-down laugh, and his eyes were wide open, looking at the things around her: the brightly coloured clothes that were so different from her own, the gloves that surely couldn't warm anyone's hands in winter; the scarves that were so soft to the touch; the bundle of papers in crabbed handwriting, tied with a ribbon; the finely cut bone combs and a dozen other things whose use she didn't know. And, of course, the big book.

She'd wanted to put them back exactly as she'd found them, with the wicker baskets that were still behind the partition, and with the wooden chest which had all the animals carved into its lid, over which she'd run her fingers, but which was too heavy to shift. Then she'd glanced into the book that she'd first ignored, thinking it would be like her father's books crammed with words and numbers, and soon she'd become engrossed in its pictures. She'd fancied herself riding with the horsemen between the green hills, travelling with the lady in blue along the carp-filled river, and flying with the thumb-sized boy on the back of a goose over snow-tipped hills, and had lost track of time. Then her father stood before her.

He didn't say anything, and kept his face turned away, as he dragged her to the parlour. He closed the door behind her with a bang and she hardly dared to move. Only when she heard the outside door open, and her father go in and out several times, did she inch to the window. Her father was in the yard, putting a burning rag to the things he'd piled up there: the things from the forbidden room. Her mother's things.

Ymke slapped her hands on the windowpane and shouted. Her father didn't listen. She rushed outside, shouting and crying, and still her father didn't turn. She hurried over to the fire, wanting to save what she could. Her father's strong hand grabbed her and pulled her away from the flames. She screamed, and flailed at him with her fists as he held her tight against him. Then, her rage dying with the fire, and only sobs remaining, he took her back inside. There, he showed her the single wooden chest with its carvings of woodland creatures.

'These will be yours, for when you're a bit older and know how to take care of them.' He opened the chest, and on top of her mother's red dress lay the big book with all the pictures.

'This was your mother's childhood favourite,' he said. 'She learned to read from it, and so shall you.'

To Be Human

'And to think that when I first saw you, I thought you were a troll.'

As soon as she said it, Ymke knew she'd made a mistake. His hand flew to his face, and his fingers touched the ridges and the red ink that spiralled around his eyes, along his nose and over his cheeks. 'And now? Am I human to you now? Or something between? A half-troll?'

He propped himself up on his elbows, and his face moved into the light of the low hanging sun. He blinked and frowned, then looked at her again.

Yes, of course you are human. The words came easily, without thinking, yet she swallowed them. She peered back at him instead, until finally she knew what she really wanted to say.

'My father is no longer young, and he's getting slower. He thinks I haven't noticed, and I let him believe that. He gets angry quickly, and later he pretends it didn't happen while I'm still boiling.'

She laid her hand on the leather binding of the book they'd been reading. 'This was my mother's. I know very little about her, except that she loved my father very much. Enough to follow him here. Out there, in the distance you know the farm of Reider Elmingha. The farmer's son is not a lot older than I am. I guess Creil is strong, yet he's not got the mind to know what strength really is. His father uses all the right words and he'll smile at you. Still, he frightens me.'

She struggled to stand up, not caring to hide the stiffness of her bad leg. Then she looked back at the giant, who lay wounded in front of their fireplace.

'You're bigger than any man I've seen, and you're covered in swirls and patterns. It's our differences that make us who we are. For good or for bad, they make us human.'

He nodded and lay back again, at ease.

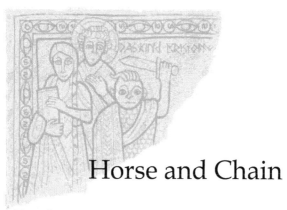

Horse and Chain

'But there you are mistaken, my dear. There is so much more to the Craft than simply treading the boards and speaking one's lines.' Master Osgot pronounced it with a capital 'C'; just a little sample of his skill. 'Those lines must be written, and they must be meaningful for the blessed audience and their author alike. Should the one who thinks up the players' parts not believe in them, then their characters would be flat, and the spectators, with their inborn cunning, would reject the whole thing.'

His glance drifted away from Kaila, to different times, other places.

'Yes, whether terror or farce is performed, it must draw in the man who stands outside that magic circle, lest interest turn to boredom and boredom to resentment. Being pelted with clods of mud is the least that can happen to the actor facing a crowd turned sour. An esteemed actor of my acquaintance, who in his day had the adulation of kings and ate off silver platters, was dragged with horse and chain out of a swineherd town when, in riper age, he only had ungainly words fed to him by an incompetent scribbler. Brrr!'

His jowls shook with the recollection. He flicked his hand, waving away the memory as if it were a horsefly.

He bent closer to Kaila. 'I was with him when he died. I was young then, and pretty, if you can believe it, and he'd been good to me. He looked awful, with wounds so deep that bone glittered wherever I washed away the blood. I tried my best to bind his wounds with strips torn off my dress. My dear, tell me: how do you mend the holes that have been beaten in a man's soul? The worst was his face, contorted like a baby's. And his sobs! They didn't cease until he died. Release could not come quick enough for him.'

'Kaila,' he gripped her shoulders, and his eyes locked onto hers, just a hand span away, 'Always make sure that you have at least one hand on your own destiny. At that young age I did not know if I would ever be a good actor. What I did know was that even a great actor is nothing when the words he speaks ring like a mallet on a lead kettle. So I read, I studied, I learned. Never for me that chain and horse!'

'At least, it won't be for the quality of your words,' Kaila finally got in. But she squeezed his hand, so he would know that what he'd told her had hit its mark.

Sebastien, Our Saviour

There was one thing Sebastien needed to do, even though Kaila was keen to hotfoot it out of Starohrad. He'd spent weeks in the castle, and while his movements had been severely restricted, he'd kept his eyes and ears open. He knew where the small doors were; the unobtrusive backdoors for the tradesmen, the hatches to throw out the slops, the dead tree leaning against the wall and used for illicit visits to servants by their lovers. He also had a fairly good idea of the routes the guards took through the castle, at which hour they were likely to get tired, and which of them finished their round quickly so they could go back to their dice and drink.

He went clad in black and, once over the castle wall, threw off his cape to reveal the white habit he'd worn for the last few weeks in the High Priestess' service. It almost fooled the servant girl who suddenly came around the corner. He assumed the well-practiced face of an innocent boy, somehow wandered off.

Her eyes narrowed. He took a step back, wondering whether to fight or flee.

'Destroy the wheel,' she whispered, gave a quick nod, and was on her way.

He crossed courtyards like a white shadow behind patrolling guards' backs and slipped through the palace's corridors, until he stood at the hated door of the Playroom. One last look over his shoulder, then he opened the door. Frightened eyes; blue eyes. A little boy started crying. Petr, of course. The door opening outside of feeding time meant that one of them was fetched and never seen again. That's how it worked. Sebastien slipped into the room and quickly closed the door behind him.

'Shush! Petr, look, it's me, Sebastien. I've come to get you away from here.'

The blonde boys in white stared at him and each other. They knew him, of course. He'd been one of them, one of the bigger boys. But, why would he take them away if 'away' meant -'Your mothers and fathers. I'll take you home,' he tried. Some careful excitement: a few boys still remembered or believed in a place like 'home'.

Then, again, the door opened. Sebastien turned around. The servant girl he'd bumped into before stood in front of him, her face flushed. Over her shoulder, he saw the guardsman. The man was a head taller than him, in full armour and with his short sword in hand. Hope drained from Sebastien. The soldier whispered something to the girl, Sebastien didn't hear what, then moved her aside and looked round the boys in the room.

'The High Priestess is gone,' he said. Then, to Sebastien: 'Let's get these children out of here.'

A Home for the Night

'Are we there yet?' Sebastien wiped the wet rag of hair from his eyes and pulled his shoe from the mud that had sucked it from his foot.

'Quit it already and watch where you're going,' Kaila called over her shoulder. She was a dozen feet ahead of him and infinitely more capable in navigating the treacherous terrain. She didn't slither away over wet mud, or nearly twist an ankle when a steppingstone gave way. She wasn't out of breath as they laboured up the hill, and didn't grab hold of each tree to have just a moment of security. She also hadn't lost her quarterstaff.

And meanwhile, the rain kept pouring down on them, turning the world beyond into a grey void.

'Are you sure it's the right way? It was going to be easy, you said.'

She held still to let him catch up. 'Yes, I'm sure. When last I was here the path was in better shape.'

What Kaila called a path, Sebastien could easily have mistaken for a small river with rapidly flowing, muddy water. And was that a dead rat that had caught against his legs, before being dragged away again?

'There were no brambles yet back then, I guess,' he muttered. Kaila had shown him how to get through them: avoid the bigger stems, flatten what's in front of you with one foot, push the rest aside with your staff. It had indeed worked, for her. The stick he'd made do with hadn't been much use.

They moved onwards, both in silence. Sebastien was too cold and miserable to speak, while Kaila had nothing to say. In this land of rain and greyness there were no shadows, yet he noticed the light slowly dimming.

'What did I tell you?' Kaila said, finally. 'We'll get a fire going and be warm and dry again in no time!' She slung her oiled leather pack off her back and removed the logs she'd dragged all the way up. Sebastian's pack, too, thudded on the dry earth of what would be their home for the night. He paced from one rock wall to the other, and back again. It took just seconds for him to come with his verdict.

'This is not even a cave. It's a - a half-cave!'

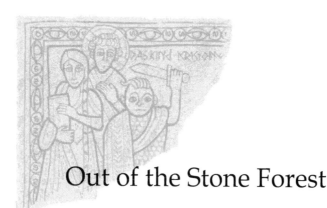

Out of the Stone Forest

The Otaswald was nothing like Ymke had expected.

It was not the stone forest of which she'd heard whispers, with trees like the columns of ancient temples. Nor did she find the mists that were said to wash over the undergrowth like an intangible sea, in which the mist-creatures wove their deceitful, magic spells.

As she guided her horse through the Otaswald, Ymke realised that the stories she'd heard were not just exaggerated; they missed the mark altogether. The ancient forest was strange indeed, but in a way that far surpassed those tales.

The trees were ancient, yes, but not as measured against the works of man. This was the forest primeval itself, with trees so imaginably old that they must have sprouted when the world was young and mankind itself still unformed. Their trunks were so broad that six men holding hands couldn't have encircled them, and their lowest branches set so high she couldn't have hit them with a thrown rock if she tried.

Whole armies could have hidden among those trees, yet she saw not a sign of a single animal: no paw print in mud, no den dug between roots, nor tufts of fur where a beast had rubbed its back against bark. It was so quiet that even her horse stepped cautiously. There was a ceaseless rushing of branches and leaves above her head, and yet she heard no birdsong.

Though it was spring, the sunlight that filtered through the dense canopy failed to warm her. But it was more than that: she felt as if the forest itself was drawing the heat from her body. While those trees around her undoubtedly were alive, the forest itself was dead. And yet, somehow, the forest was hungry. She drew her cloak tighter around her and spurred her horse on.

At last, the trees opened before her. The ground ahead sloped up towards the gigantic rock outcrop of the Otasfaust. On its crown lay the city of Otasring, whose inhabitants had fled the forest centuries before her. With the welcome heat of the spring sun, relief flooded through her body.

The Child Asleep

Deep in the night, Kaila and Ymke discussed what glorious miracles the Child would perform over the course of the following days. Sitting close together on the bed, they spoke softly, as in the next room the Child himself slept. At long last, their talk petered out. Ymke yawned.

'Can I get you anything from the kitchen, Kai? I'm getting the bed-stone.' She'd been on her feet so much more than she had in long time, and an ache had settled deep into her hip. The heated stone, wrapped in linen, brought her the relief she needed to fall asleep.

'It's okay. I'll get it,' Kaila said, and hopped out of bed. She padded round the bed, with her lover's eyes on her.

'Kai,' Ymke hissed. A sheet tossed over, and nakedness covered, Kaila opened the door. Before she'd even set a foot outside the bedroom, she held still again.

'Come, you don't want to miss this,' she whispered. Ymke too left the bed, and Kaila enveloped her in the sheet, letting her lean on her strong shoulder.

'Look at him. The hopes and expectations of so many people rest on him. You and me, we've asked so much of him, and yet he's played his role so well. It's so easy to forget that he's really still a young boy, isn't it?'

Now Ymke saw it too, in the light of the dying fire. In the oblivion of sleep Sebastien's face had settled into an innocence that was different from the studied purity of the Child's. His lips were slightly parted, and his left hand, close to his face, was open. In it he held a small toy, crudely carved from wood. If there ever had been paint on the gnome with the pointed hat, it had long been worn off by the touch of a boy's hand over thousands of nights.

The Kindness of Neighbours

It had taken Ymke a lot of time building up trust with the old priest before he would finally speak in anything but the vaguest hints about the death of his ward, the Uncomplaining Child. She realised it was a story he would narrate with great enthusiasm, once a certain ritual of coaxing and flattery had been observed; a ritual she'd had to uncover as she interviewed him those past weeks. And so, she followed the slight hints the old man left for her, like seeds luring a chicken to the block.

'-And then, of course, as if the poor child had not suffered enough, they put a torch to the Wheel. I stayed close to him, and I think he saw me. I like to think it gave him a measure of comfort to see a familiar face. It's tempting to say it was bravery that kept me there, but, and it shames me to say, I feared that if I fled, I'd draw attention to myself. People are so fickle. One day they are your friends, and the next - '

The old man shook his head and fell silent. Ymke looked up from her notes, and hoped that her face showed the right mixture of understanding and encouragement. He closed his eyes and a sigh came from deep inside him.

'The smell. That is what was worst of all. It is indescribable, yet it will never leave my nostrils. It will always haunt me. It is -'

He was distracted by a stout woman who came striding towards them, a covered pot in her hands. Father Folkhert seldom had to worry about dinner; as his neighbours took pride in providing for him by turns. He sat up straight and clapped his hands together. Ymke knew that her audience for the day was over; there would be no more seeds for her to peck.

'Frau Dankwert!' the old man cried out. 'What a welcome sight you are for my rheumy eyes. What is it you bring me today?'

She leaned towards the old man and uncovered the pot. Father Folkhert bent forward and sniffed. He smiled broadly.

'Roast pig! What a treat!'

Fireflies

'How did you know?'

It was a sultry evening, and what warmth they still needed, sitting on the small, wooden footbridge, they got from each other.

'Know what?' Kaila asked.

'You know, in the inn, when we first met.' Ymke pulled her closer. Burying her face in Kaila's black hair, she breathed in. No perfume, no artificial scent, just... Kaila. Kaila's hands were on hers, and her strong fingers softly squeezed.

'I liked the look of you, so I threw my line out. That's what you do on the road with the army, or alone; wondering what if' will inevitably turn into 'could have' when you don't grab the bull by the horns. Or the cow, as the case may be.'

For that, Ymke slapped her on the head, but not hard, and then kissed it better anyway.

'And you? Would you have known?'

'Yes. Maybe not immediately, and I don't quite know how it works... see those fireflies?' Kaila did. 'It's like that. Perhaps people behave just a little bit differently when they feel attraction to someone, or are available. Maybe it's even in the way they talk. They may not even mean to do it. For me it's as if they start glowing, but without giving off light. Strange, isn't it?'

'Not really.' Kaila pulled Ymke's arm tighter around her, and kissed her hand. 'And me, did I glow?'

'Honey, you blinded me.'

Across the River

The river wasn't very wide, yet the opposite bank was barely visible, and a vicious rain whipped their faces. Hooves skittered on wet boards as Kaila led the last of their horses off the pontoon. She pushed the unwilling beast onto the slimy mud, shouted at it, and cursed when she herself slipped and fell. As she scrambled away from the pounding hooves, Ymke grabbed the horse's reins. She tugged gently and spoke to it calmly, though her words got lost in the storm. Sebastien noticed that her limp was worse than usual. He made a half-hearted gesture towards them, offering to help, but backed off eagerly when Kaila hissed at him.

'I'll settle with the ferryman, then,' he called to them, and added: 'I know my place.' They didn't hear him, engaged as they were with the horse and each other.

The tall man in his long, weather-beaten coat of tough leather still stood where he had throughout the crossing, with one hand on the thick rope that spanned from one shore to the other, and his eyes on the invisible horizon. Lank grey hair hung beneath the water-laden brim of his hat, and the thin, wet tangles clung to his shoulders and back when he turned his head towards the boy.

'A denarius for each of us, plus one and a half per horse; wasn't that what it said on the sign?' Sebastien repeated himself, loudly, when the man seemed not to hear him over the wind and rain. 'What if we make it a round seven?' After all, the crossing had not been pleasant, and Kaila had done all of the pulling.

The ferryman's grooved face disappeared as he bent his head. Then he looked up at Sebastien, with eyes that bored deep into the boy's mind. He pointed at the rotting stool that was the only furniture on the flat boat. On it sat a tin plate, with a haze above it from the hard rain bouncing off a handful of coins.

'Too lazy even to pick up your previous fares,' Sebastien muttered. He thought of 'clinking the coin', making the sound of putting down money without leaving any. *Not worth it,* he decided. *It'd be just when the old bastard comes to life.* He shrugged and paid the full price for himself, the women and their horses. Then he carefully walked the gangplank to the bank, careful to avoid the worst of the mud churned up by horse and friend alike.

While their horses grazed on the sparse grass at the riverside, Kaila and Ymke sat huddled under a tree, for what little shelter it gave them. They'd pulled the hoods of their travelling cloaks deeply over their faces, trying to keep their hard tack from getting soaked. They reminded Sebastien of mossy boulders, one smaller than the other but also, he knew, much stronger.

'Daddy Longlegs there couldn't be more of a scary ferryman type if he tried!' He wiped the wet locks of hair away from his eyes and sat down next to them. He stared at the ferry, slowly retreating, swallowed by the rain. He could just make out the ferryman, pulling it along the rope hand-over-hand. 'Where does he think he is? The Death River?'

'What's that about the Death River?' Kaila followed his glance down the river.

'That boatman,' Sebastien replied. 'As if you have to look like death warmed up, to work one of these boats. Just standing there, staring at us. He should be at home, tending the daisies, if not pushing them! I can't believe I paid full price. I must be slipping.'

Kaila shrugged her hood back a bit to look up at him, her eyebrows raised. Ymke smiled.

'What?' Kaila asked. 'The ferryman? On the boat just now?'

'Yes, of course I'm talking about that ferryman. Do you think it's normal having men on these boats who won't say a word to you and won't even lift a finger to get you to the other side?'

Kaila laughed. 'Sebastien, you're cute, but don't try that one with me. There is no ferryman!'

Sebastien peered at the ferry. A milky shaft of light wrestled through the clouds overhead, and caught it as it drifted ever so slowly across the river - with not a soul on board.

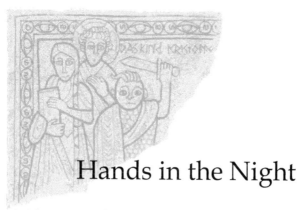

Hands in the Night

'- They came from underground, and they howled. The sound was enough to drive him mad.' Sebastien raised the tankard of ale to his mouth. He was finished with his story.

They had put several weeks' travel between them and Otasfaust, and its surrounding forest with those enormous, ancient trees had slowly become a mere shadow in their minds. They were lucky to have found a hostel before the weather turned against them, and while the storm raged outside, with shutters groaning and willow branches beating against the weathered wood, they amused themselves with stories of ghosts and monsters they'd heard on their travels, before they found each other.

'And these *boggards,* you say, were the reason they built their city on the Otasfaust?' Ymke swirled her drink, imagining the procession of hundreds of men, women and children, with their beasts and wagons, forging themselves a path up that enormous rock.

'I don't buy it, Kaila said. 'They don't sound that impressive to me. Creatures that are nothing more than heads and hands. They could just have stomped on them. *Splotch!*'

She signalled to the innkeeper, made a circular movement with one finger and stuck up three others. He shook his head and went back to wiping glasses. The wind moaned in the chimney pipe and drew red flames from the exhausted wood. The night was winding down.

'I think our host wants to go to bed, and so do I.' Ymke stood up and rubbed her leg. 'The soreness is easing off, which means it will be a better day tomorrow, or that I've numbed it into submission. Either way, I'm making the most of it and turning in.'

She squeezed Kaila's shoulder in passing and told her not to make it too late, then walked down the hall to their room.

'Boggards! *Splotch* indeed!' she said, and laughed. And yet, she made sure that when she undressed, her bare feet did not touch the floor, just in case a floorboard should lift, and probing fingers find their way towards her.

The wine made her sleep fitful, her dreams laced with grasping fingers like brittle sticks, and a scream trapped in her throat. When searching hands did find her, she knew their warmth, their callouses, their care. Her fingers reached out in return, and found Kaila.

That Most Precious

A sombre keep between one point and another is where I live now. It would not be in any way remarkable, were it not the only inhabited place between the Dadjo plateau and Gobari. Few men cross the desert between these outposts of human civilisation: only those who have a wish to die, or those who have such a strong wish to live that they would rather face the unending sands than whatever death is chasing them.

Those that do not leave their bones to wither in that merciless, vast nothing will inevitably come to our fortress. I say 'our', but it's not mine, nor that of my fellows. It has not been anyone's for so long that none of us really knows who originally built it, or for what purpose. Its walls are thick and built from stones hauled over many leagues. They keep out the worst heat of the day and the cold of night, and also protect our hoard.

No army has ever come for our treasure, nor bands of robbers. Whoever wants to partake of it is free to do so, as free as anyone who wants to add to it. Our fortress guards not coin or jewel, but that most precious resource of all: knowledge. That is what I came for, some years ago, when I escaped from a life which was not really life at all, and a death that would surely have followed quickly. They took me in and – again, I say 'they', which would imply a group to which one can belong or not belong. Everyone is free to come and free to go, without any questions being asked, as long as the few rules of the fortress are obeyed. Its first rule is 'do not judge,' and for that I am happy.

When I had healed from my journey and made known my wish to stay, I was appointed a cell. It's simple and small, yet it is enough for me, and so much more than I've had before: it has a door that opens and closes as I wish. There I spent my nights in sleep and contemplation, while I spend my days reading, copying and cataloguing the books and manuscripts that are in our keeping.

How long I will stay, I do not know. My brothers are still unfree in those cold, grim lands far away. They are in the back of my mind, always, while I study and learn, until I know what to do.

The Amazon's Lament

'The Fury with the Axe,' they call me. I've roamed the land for a score of years, fighting, reaving, waging war. My strength and my sure hand with a weapon are the gift, or curse, of the Goddess. No man may possess me, unless he bests me in combat.

Today he appeared. I knew him as soon as I saw him. Our steel clashed from sun-up to dusk, until he had me on my back, my battle axe discarded.

'The spell is broken – claim your prize!' I said to him.

'No, old woman, I'll not have you,' he said, and turned his back.

Once more he looked round at how he'd left me, without my powers and without my pride.

Then, through my tears I saw him frown. I'd let him win, yes, but I knew what I myself had gained. I was alone; the Goddess had gone from me. Yet, for the first time in my life, I was free.

Thank you

For buying *The Red Man and Others*.

If you enjoyed this book
please rate or review it at:
https://linktr.ee/turniplanterns

To contact us, or join our mailing list
please visit our blog:
http://turniplanterns.wordpress.com

The Making Of

In which the magicians reveal the trap door in the table, how the cards are marked, and where the pigeons are hidden in their sleeves - to say nothing of how the sausage is made.

The titular figure from *The Red Man* came to me more than two decades ago, on a train ride to my parents, up in the north of the Netherlands. My note of the time is titled 'The Red Butchers,' and I describe them as 'giant, muscled men, put in the front ranks of battles.' They'd be difficult to miss: 'Aside from their size, for which they're bred, because of the tattoos covering them completely. These, mainly red, tattoos make them into living flags, but also strike fear into the opponents. They also hide scars and any wounds they'd sustain.'

I thought this would make an interesting contribution to a shared Fantasy universe I was asked to work on by a novice publisher. Nothing came of it, as one of the publishers was a law student and presented me with a fist-thick contract. Diligently going through it with my red pen I made the following conclusions: 1) Payment of any work would only happen on publication. 2) Submitted artwork would be owned by the publisher. 3) Having material held by the publisher meant sharing its financial liability.

My conclusion was that I could send them a drawing, they could put it in a drawer with no intent to actually use it, but meanwhile have me on the books as someone to carry the can if things went wrong. I showed the contract to a friend who worked in publishing, and his advice was: 'These guys are pirates. Don't go to sea with them.' I think I may already have had an inkling, as I'd made a note, sitting in the train on my way up north, to present them with 'nothing actually publishable.'

While the whole of the country is flat, there is a marked change once you come up north; sand and peat ground give way to clay, and clumps of pine forest to wide expanses of grass and farmland. The big farms with the ornate farmhouses close to the Wadden Sea coast, in the area called Het Hogeland, testify to the fertility of the sea clay. Whole communities grew up around these farms, who would recognise the farmer as their lord and master, in a near-feudal society whose last echoes were still noticeable when I was a child in the '80s. Especially when, like me, you were regarded as coming 'from labourer stock.'

The farms Sunne and Mone, owned by the Elmingha family in *The Red Man*, are like these farms. In naming them I was thinking of farms like those owned in the area by the Teenstra family in the eighteenth and nineteenth centuries. The Teenstras were involved with reclaiming land and agricultural innovation, prime proponents of the Enlightenment in the northern farming communities, until disease, natural disaster and a financial crash all but wiped out their fortunes.

The most famous son of this family, Marten Douwes Teenstra, had to sell his farm, and earned a living as colonial administrator, writer and busy body. Aside from his recently cleaned up gravestone, there is not a monument to be found to him. The memory of the Ulrummer is long, and he remains unforgiven for heckling Ulrum's favourite son, the anti-Enlightenment preacher Hendrik de Cock.

While the northern provinces of Groningen and Friesland now seem peaceful, tranquil even, it hasn't always been like that. While the vast majority have been demolished and the remaining few show little of their original shape, old maps show the countryside littered with strongholds, called 'borg' or 'börg' in Groningen and 'stins' in Friesland. There were hundreds of them, used as places of refuge in times of danger.

Violence didn't only come from within, though, as the Eighty Years' War, against the Spanish, also reached the northern provinces. In 1576 the fortification Zoutkamp was built on the coast, for a Spanish garrison to guard the Reitdiep river that ran to the city of Groningen. In the late eighteenth century the bulwarks, by then dilapidated, were repaired to guard French-occupied Holland from an English attack from the sea. Though 80-100 German soldiers occupied Zoutkamp in the Second World War, the area was relatively quiet, though a lot of small injustices were noticed but unreported thanks to a prevailing attitude of 'listen and watch, but keep silent'.

While my dad's family came through the war reasonably well, my mom's family was not so lucky. They're from what we'd call 'across the water,' separated from the rest of the province by the Reitdiep river, and speaking a version of the Gronings dialect that owes more to the Frisian language. Her birthplace is also removed from the fertile clay; closer to peat country where the farms were small and the people poor.

This is where my grandfather had a small shop. In 1943 a British bomber in trouble accidentally dropped his bombs early: not over the North Sea, but right on top of the house. Grandfather pushed in a newly built wall with his back, and everyone escaped from the burning house unscathed. However, they'd lost everything, and when my mother was born, in the autumn of 1945, it was at the farm of her aunt.

There's a photo from the mid-1950s of my grandparents and their children. My grandmother looks tired, my grandfather sad and defeated. Some of their adult children smile and others don't, but the only person who seems happy is my mom, then aged ten. She probably doesn't know yet what the rest know: that the family portrait is being made before the inevitable happens – my grandmother has cancer. When my grandmother died a few years later, my mother had lost that innocence, and her childhood was truly done when, soon after, she was told by her father that she'd be going 'to the farmer' to work as junior maid. She was taken out of school and placed in a part-time housekeeping school until she was fifteen. Marriage, for many of these women, was the only way to escape what amounted to indentured servitude.

My grandfather made many bad decisions in his long life, many through stubbornness. The worst was probably deciding, when my mother was born with hip dysplasia, that she didn't need medical treatment, and would surely grow out of it. Though she spent part of her later childhood in a brace, the situation by then was not fully reversible, causing her a lifetime of pain and difficulty walking.

There's a photo of my grandfather as a child, with his parents and older sisters – a small, wide-eyed boy with shoes that are too big, surrounded by stern parents and forbidding-looking young women. That little boy never left him, I think. I'm constantly revising my opinion of the old man though, and I've ended up with a picture of a man who was constantly out of his depth. My mother says that he could be very kind, but I never knew him to smile. Just once, caught at the very edge of a photo, he laughs, when he thinks himself invisible.

Kaila and Sebastien roam, which allows us to bring them to various situations and settings. The city of Starohrad is a cross between Edinburgh and Prague, two of my favourite cities, and both of them divided. Edinburgh has its crammed Old Town with its several levels and piled-up buildings, and then on the other side of the valley, New Town, where the better off moved once the city really was bursting at the seams. This is where Scottish writer R.L. Stevenson grew up, but it was in the underbelly of Old Town that he spent his days as a student. You can find both faces of Edinburgh, literally and figuratively, in his *Strange Case of Dr Jekyll and Mr Hyde*.

Prague is split in two by the Vltava river, its two sides joined by the Charles Bridge with its thirty Baroque statues. Go just a little bit off the beaten path, and you'll find yourself in crooked alleys and passages that'll give you the feeling that you've fallen back in time. Like Edinburgh, Prague has a castle that towers over the city, though its castle's ornate buildings with their yellow stone and red roofs are very little like Scotland's grey colossus. Many years ago, when I was on holiday in Prague, they were just preparing the castle for the yearly Summer Shakespeare Festival. I'd be gone by the time they performed *Macbeth*, but at least I came home with a poster, one of those wonderful examples of Eastern European poster art.

The stage they were building in the castle was much like the two-level stage from the time of Shakespeare, and it was too tempting not to use it in our story. We got details on the stage and stagecraft of the era from James Shapiro's *1599: A Year in the Life of William Shakespeare*. I can also recommend his follow-up, *Contested Will: Who Wrote Shakespeare?* Spoiler: it was William Shakespeare. The book makes mincemeat of the theory that a 'commoner' like Shakespeare could never have written such plays. (On which note: don't believe that Leonardo painted Mary Magdalene in his *Last Supper*, or that artist Walter Sickert was Jack the Ripper.)

The leader of our troupe of actors is modelled on Oscar Wilde, albeit by way of actor-writer-presenter Stephen Fry. Fry did a splendid job portraying Wilde in the 1997 film, and I'd always hoped for a post-Reading Gaol sequel, for example based on Peter Ackroyd's *The Last Testament of Oscar Wilde*. Rupert Everett's *The Happy Prince* fills that hole admirably, but just as someone can have 'their' James Bond, Stephen Fry's is 'my' Oscar. And that's how I wrote the character: I imagine him as warmer and less sneering than the real Oscar Wilde. Up to the last draft he was called Master Hosker, and we had the hardest time coming up with another name. 'Hoscard?' I proposed at one time, but was pointed out that it was just 'Oscar', sandwiched between an *H* and a *d*.

The High Priestess Lisanna, meanwhile, wasn't based on anybody in particular, though her decadence can easily be found in the history books. One we found very useful was Frances Stonor Saunders's *Hawkwood: Diabolical Englishman*, about the fourteenth century mercenary John Hawkwood, who fought in the Hundred Years' War, then became a much sought-after *condottieri* in Italy. An example was given of King Edward III, with his son the Black Prince, returning to London from France. The bells pealed all day, and an escort of a thousand mounted men guided him to Westminster: 'From twelve suspended gilded cages provided by the goldsmiths of London, maidens scattered flowers of gold and silver filigree over the cavalcade.' Reading this, we figured that we needed to crank up the decadence of Lisanna's court.

We'd pegged Kaila as a fighter, but we didn't know much more about her. What we did know was that we didn't want any as-broad-as-they-are-tall dwarfs like Tolkien's or, god forbid, the *Gotrek and Felix* books. Then I was introduced to a young woman who had just joined the Turkish team at work. When I was sitting down and she was standing, she looked me straight in the eye. 'You're going to be Gandalf at Hallowe'en, and I'll be Frodo,' she said. It was quickly decided that our Kaila would be from her world's equivalent of the Middle East, and like my colleague she'd be small, but not a dwarf.

That my colleague turned out to have been in the army I considered a good omen.

Just as important for us in figuring out who Kaila was going to be was finding Samantha Wright's Instragram page. As PixieStrength, she chronicles her journey from Olympic-class weightlifter to a healthier way of working with her body. It'll be clear how she contributed a lot to Kaila's physical shape, but she also influenced Kaila's development into a more three-dimensional character. When dubbed 'cutest weightlifter,' she noted that behind those words lay an implicit irony, while 'contrary to that implication, the qualities, beauty and strength, are not antithetic. They are harmonious.' Alongside the photos and videos of her working out, Samantha shares her pain, and the trauma she endured. In sharing her vulnerability too, she shows real strength and courage; more so than any fighter on a winning streak could.

And then Sebastien. You'll not miss the mark if you picture a teenage version of comedian James Acaster. To be honest, we haven't figured out quite who he is, or where he came from. There are stories to be told here, but the stories Sebastien will tell about himself are probably not the truth. I doubt Sebastien is even the boy's real name.

The people who'd object to Kaila and Ymke's romance might also not be too happy with how religion is treated in the story. Father Folkert comes out of it pretty well; he has an innate goodness and faith which (eventually) supersede religious dogma. Then again, if he started off as an ineffectual, doddery old man, it became clear to us during the writing process that he hadn't stayed alive by being anyone's fool. Folkhert clearly is not happy with the hijacking of religion by groups of – let's be honest – bully boys, and I believe that he found in our trio a stick to properly stir up some trouble. As I write this in Northern Ireland, despite a decades old peace process, criminal gangs masquerading as freedom fighters, on both sides, are still terrorising their own people and their alleged enemies.

In our story, there clearly is a need for the Child. As with Father Folkert, it hardly matters whether Sebastien really is the Child come back, or just a symbol of what they believe in. Despite our poking fun with the multitude of skulls of the Child, and his baby teeth, relics do give people a focus for their belief. Just as nobody would mistake a little bronze Christ on a little wooden cross for the real thing, I'm not sure whether people, deep inside, really would believe that the crown of thorns that was rescued from the Notre Dame fire was really worn by Jesus. The Baltic rush, of which the circlet is woven, is native to Northern Britain, the Baltic and Scandinavia. To find it on the head of a carpenter in first century Judea would be a miracle indeed!

It does make you think: if there was such a person as Jesus, Son of God, and he were to return – would he be welcomed? Would he soon be found inconvenient by the church leaders, whose dogma he would no doubt reject? I imagine him permanently frustrated, flipping over tables in many a church, temple and cathedral. Just imagine him finding out about the prosperity gospel! And would the Church hierarchy then decide that he'd serve their purpose best by taking up his appointed place on the cross once more?

After the previous setting of Starohrad we were looking for a location for a new story. According to Lotte Eisner's book, *The Haunted Screen,* German Expressionist films had been referred to as *Landschaft mit Seele,* landscape with a soul. While not mentioned in the same breath as the Expressionist films *Das Cabinet des Dr. Caligari,. Nosferatu* and *Der Golem,* the world of *Die Nibelungen* definitely is one of artifice. I took the visual cues of the first of the *Nibelungen* films, *Siegfried,* and reverse engineered a pseudo-mythology for the people of Otasring. The forest with its mammoth trees, through which both Siegfried and Ymke travel, the city's architecture with its cyclopean walls, but also the characters in Fritz Lang's movie, with their stylized movements and (to borrow a phrase from elsewhere) 'gigantic melancholies and gigantic mirth' are the people who inhabit our story.

This is a world which in reality couldn't quite exist, and it seems sometimes as if Kaila and Ymke realise this. This allows them to move between the squares on the city's game boards, and subvert its *gründlichkeit* for their own gain and survival.

The shorter pieces in this book are the products of October 2019, when I used an Inktober prompts card to write a series of vignettes. They do not always work as stand-alone stories, but offer interpolations, sojourns and the tying off of loose ends. They were a lot of fun to do; some of the vignettes I wrote have been combined, some will be absorbed in stories yet to come. Others we've given some spit and polish and present to you here.

We've got a folder in our shared drive with ideas for more Kaila and Sebastian stories. There's a prologue story about how Kaila became a swordswoman, Master Osgot might make a comeback in a ghost story, ghosts (less literal) from the past come back to haunt Sebastien, and there is an assortment of fragments and notions that are also coalescing into some stories that surprise even ourselves. The roots of 'The Fury with the Axe' in *The Amazon's* Lament will be clear; I always wondered what happens with characters like Red Sonja when they get older; one day their luck must run out. This woman will make a return in something we're still working on, and which folds her neatly into the chronology of our adventurers. We hope you'll be along for the ride!

Remco

In *The Red Man*, Ymke's story starts with a threatening world, seen through a tiny aperture. She doesn't yet realise how much an isolated upbringing and a tiny family have limited her perspective - any more than I did at her age. By the end of *The Return of the Uncomplaining Child*, that world is no less threatening, but she's learned to deal with it on her own terms. Likewise, she's had to define who she is, because identity is precarious when you grow up in the long shadow of a parent's absence.

Remco and I decided that Ymke's parents had been star-crossed lovers who'd run away from some easier life because being together mattered more than material security. That fell apart for them in a tragic yet mundane way, death being no respecter of people's dreams. One thing I've always loved about historical (and quasi-historical fantasy) fictional settings is that it's common for characters to be motherless, fatherless, or both. In real life, my birth story (my dad and I missed each other by two days) is a conversation stopper. In fiction, losing a parent is commonplace, a wound often transmuted into a source of strength.

At the same time, people around me went through worse losses. Nobody took my father from me. I rarely had reason to truly fear other people. But everyone who grew up in Northern Ireland during those years, and during our complicated peace since then, has been affected by the conflict. And in every conflict, there are people who have to exist in the middle of it, just trying to go about their everyday lives. The Troubles were, in a very background way, my frame of reference for the civil war burning around Ymke's farm in *The Red Man*. Religious extremism here in Northern Ireland explains everything about the Wheelies. But for *The Return of the Uncomplaining Child*, we needed a way to bring Ymke and Kaila together. I grew up in a place small enough that my head turns if I hear the accent in a foreign country, so language felt like the natural way to connect them, and it felt plausible that the mercenary life might have taken Kaila to Ymke's homeland.

Insular places have their shibboleths and their unstated rules. Ymke prefers not to know who Kaila fought for because that would mean - for both of them - taking a position on the causes of the conflict; something Ymke's people have learned not to do, because they are all mutually harmed by a war perpetuated by distant rival dukes. That was a wishful inversion on my part of the Northern Irish habit of figuring out a stranger's religious and community affiliation (and thereby making a whole set of assumptions about their politics) based on what, to outsiders, might seem like very innocent questions. There's good faith in the way Ymke and Kaila approach each other: a good faith that I try, and sometimes fail, to extend to people as life throws us together.

Ymke is not a woman of action by inclination, and the contrast between her and Kaila - entirely without my meaning it to - dramatises a problem I think about a lot. I grew up on action, science fiction and fantasy films and I always assumed that if something violent and dangerous happened, I'd be the practical, even ruthless person who took down an assailant twice my size, fetched help or stood up to injustice. Events have taught me that my innate response to violence is that my legs turn to jelly. It turns out I'm not Sarah Connor after all, and my physical disability only magnifies that vulnerability. Ymke's rebellions, like mine, have often been subtle ones: staying alive in a world that oppresses disabled people is also a form of resistance. But sometimes we're both surprised by what we're capable of doing when we really have to - and with the right person by our side.

Angeline

Speculative Fiction Showcase Interview

In October last year Jessica Rydill interviewed us for the Speculative Fiction Showcase, which is a blog dedicated to indie Science Fiction, Fantasy and Horror. You can find this interview, and many others, at http://indiespecfic.blogspot.com

To begin with, please you tell us about your story collection
The Red Man and Others.

The Red Man and Others is second world fantasy with plucky outsiders who aim to survive in a world that underestimates them. We meet Kaila, a small but tough mercenary; Sebastien, a young con artist who's used to getting by on charm; and Ymke, a scribe who's escaped a childhood war to find love with Kaila. Together, they're out to take down a cult, the Brotherhood of the Wheel, and right some social wrongs while they're at it.

Originally, we'd written *The Red Man* (Ymke's story) and *Road to Starohrad* (where Kaila and Sebastien meet) as unconnected stories. We planned for Kaila and Sebastien to be sort of a double act in *The Return of the Uncomplaining Child*. We found that we needed a third character, a scribe, and it immediately made sense that Ymke had wandered southward and established herself in the city on the rock. And before we knew it, she and Kaila were a couple, and poor Sebastien found himself sleeping on the bare wooden floor.

You describe *The Red Man and Others* as a Sword and Sorcery collection. Why was it important for you to write in this genre, and how does the book differ from traditional Sword and Sorcery novels?

Sword and Sorcery is about living in a fundamentally dangerous world, but one where you can survive because you have your weapon and your wits. That's attractive when you live in a complex modern society (also a dangerous place for many of us), even when you agree with that society's consensus that we solve conflict through discussion rather than sword fights.

Of course, that consensus is hugely flexible and tends to favour the wealthy and powerful - violence happens to someone, somewhere. So, the genre also speaks to the part of us that hungers for justice, in whatever form. But Sword and Sorcery is more than just an unreconstructed guilty pleasure: it's about finding the autonomy and inner resources to survive. Escapism, but also nourishment.

Depending on which audience we find ourselves speaking to, we confess to writing Sword & Sorcery, or call it Heroic Fantasy. While obviously we're fans of the genre, we're also aware of the stigma that is attached to it: 1980s VHS tapes, with guys so packed with muscles that they can hardly move, rescuing barely legal girls in strips of white silk; paperback covers in oil paint and oiled biceps and babes. From the late '60s onwards, Conan readers were reassured in the intro that they wouldn't find any feminists or angry Black people in their comfort reading, and half a century later it's something that a contingent of fans still wants to cling to: stories for and about manly white men who are manly and white, and women who know their place.

We believe that the genre should be accessible to readers of all demographics. There's an active and pretty vocal group within S&S fandom who seek to drag it back or keep it chained to its roots in the '30s or resurgence in the '60s. They hang on to an idealisation of toxic masculinity that others are trying to leave behind. They think they are creating a safe haven, but what they get is a ghetto. Luckily, there are many, including white men, who do want to move on.

Tell us about your protagonists - sell-sword Kaila, teenage con-artist Sebastien and Ymke, who lives with her father in the

war-torn north of Cruoningha. Who are they and what drives them?

These three characters are none of them conventional Sword and Sorcery figures. While we did make use of familiar Fantasy tropes, we gave them a slant or inverted them. With Kaila and Sebastien, for example, we took the trope of the big guy travelling with an innocent young girl and turned that into a very small woman who travels with a young boy, who isn't quite innocent. In the titular story Ymke does meet her Big Strong Guy, but we've upended the trope in another way there.

Kaila ran away from everything she knew at fifteen, because she saw no future in conforming to traditional roles. As a very small woman she will always be underestimated, and proving herself has made her brave and independent - to a fault. She surprises herself by taking Sebastien under her wing. He's a would-be ruthless kid with a heart, who is looking to belong.

Ymke, meanwhile, has grown up in isolation, with her father teaching her to hide and be afraid, because she's disabled and lives in a war zone. She feels that a lot has been kept from her: knowledge of her late mother, a family secret, the chance to be part of the world.

Collectively, these stories are about interdependence, and we're very fond of using the term 'found family'; while bonds of blood can be strong, the bonds of friendship and love are stronger, as these are the people you choose to be with rather than the ones fate, for better or worse, saddles you with.

How easy - or difficult - was it for you to write a book together?

It helped that we'd spent years doing freelance arts journalism together, and also that we never envisaged quite how big the whole *Red Man* project would become. We had short story ideas which grew together, and we've been writing together for fifteen years, in one way or another, so we've evolved a process of doing drafts by turns which works for us.

Angeline: We have complementary strengths. Remco is brilliant at generating ideas, and at plotting, while I have an ear for dialogue and I like figuring out how relationships work, so the things one of us gets stuck on are usually not so opaque to the other. We don't tend to have major differences about story direction, and where we differ about character motivations, it's a matter of nuance rather than complete contrasts, so we're both steering the ship, but we agree on the bearings. Our writing styles don't differ too much, and have grown closer, and we're almost pastiching each other's tone at times. After several passes, when we're particularly happy with a certain bit of writing, we often can no longer make out which of us came up with it.

Remco: The advantage is that we can both be critics, troubleshooters and editors while we're in the process, and can bounce ideas and drafts off each other. At WorldCon 2019 in Dublin, Peter Morwood and Diane Duane were in a panel about writing couples. They talked about writing *Sword of Xanten*, a *Nibelungen* film, and how they wrote a beginning scene of different rods of steel turned and welded together into a sword. That's a pretty good analogy for how we write. We each bring our skills, and then we forge and hammer until it's not two bars of steel, but a single sword. Sharp, we hope.

Please tell us more about the original art for the book.

Remco: We'd both agreed for a long time that when we would write a book, I'd illustrate it. I've got a background in the arts, studied at the art academy in Utrecht (The Netherlands) and had been illustrating for Dutch SFF magazines for many years, eventually experimenting with Photoshop, puppets and 3D set-ups. Drawing and painting has always been very personal for me – it's something I've done since I was very young, and 'he does art' became part of who I was.

About a decade ago, having emigrated to Northern Ireland, I painted a few portraits for an arts magazine here, and was really hoping that this would be a reboot of my artistic endeavours. One, a portrait of Anne Rice, was for the cover, and the other was to be a full-page spread. For some reason, the second portrait was printed over one column, right next to a photo of the same person in the same pose, and Anne Rice's portrait was bumped off the cover by Stephenie Meyer: the publisher had decided that readers want good-looking young women. Anne Rice appeared postage stamp sized on the contents page.

So, I hadn't really been doing any art since then, not seriously, and had to really awaken my drawing hand again. I started with small thumbnails on typing paper. With an old book on Prague next to me, the model for Starohrad, I made lots of doodles of buildings, city-scapes, and especially statues. Baroque sculpture is perfect for this sort of thing – they're very dramatic, and as I didn't want overly realistic drawings, the exaggerated poses invited me to push even further. Even so, when I did the first lot of final drawings, I put them aside as they were weak and fiddly, and I felt they needed to be more dramatic.

I usually draw with pencil on A3, and go over it with pen and ink. Then I usually get out the brush, a really beat up little thing, to 'mess it up' with some heavy black lines. This is where the drawing gets weight, and I push it away from becoming too mannered. I usually wash in grey with watered down ink, and then I bring in more detail with white paint and ink. When I've pulled all the chaos back to something appealing again, I scan it in, and do the last tweaks in Photoshop.

Angeline, what influences have you brought to your writing? You mention your experience growing up disabled - what does that mean for you as a writer?

Angeline: I became chronically ill when I was nine, left traditional education early and, as we only learned recently, I'm autistic. I have Crohn's disease, Short Bowel Syndrome and Intestinal Failure, and I've relied on tube feeding of different kinds since my teens. My education was disrupted and finally derailed by a series of major operations that took up a lot of my late teens and my twenties, so I emerged as a freelance writer in 2008 with the qualifications of a 16-year-old and less confidence. I didn't know I was autistic or that it was making the interpersonal parts of freelancing – pitching by phone, interviewing people in person – tougher, and while I'm proud of what Remco and I achieved in our work then, in time it was a relief to focus on the fiction.

So, I look at the social world as an outsider by both nature and experience. Ymke's perspective is therefore very grounded in mine: like me she has a parent she can't remember, she's missed a lot of the normal, formative social experiences, and she's hungry to absorb everything that she can of the world.

I gravitate to outsiders as friends and as fictional subjects - all three of our protagonists are people who have never quite fitted wherever they were, but together, that becomes a thing they have in common and a source of strength, and that has been my experience of connecting with other disabled people, and other marginalised people in general.

On a purely practical level, my productivity fluctuates enormously. When I have the energy and focus to write, I have to really go for it and not let other things get in the way. It's enormously frustrating, and figuring out how to get the most out of my time and energy is an ongoing project.

Remco, you mention the importance of your heritage to your writing. Tell us about this, and how the place where you grew up influenced your creative imagination.

Remco: I'm from the north of the province of Groningen, hardly disguised in *The Red Man* as Cruoningha, from a village called Ulrum. Once it would have been close to the sea, but over the last few centuries the sea has been pushed back about 15 miles. It's still a very agricultural area, with a strong sense of identity and culture which is different from surrounding areas. Up until a couple of centuries ago, it really was the arse-end of nowhere, and to reach the city from Ulrum took half a day's travel by barge, as there were no decent roads.

It's very quiet there, and when you stand outside of the village you can see the other villages on the horizon. The area has a bloody past, though: as the main waterway from the sea to Groningen led through it, it was of strategic importance, so any time the Netherlands was at war, with Germany, France, or Spain, the countryside suffered. Even 'friendly' soldiers in the deeper past weren't always a blessing – if they were not quartered with you, and eating your stores, they'd engage in a bit of plundering to supplement their mercenary's wages. Oh, and then there was the civil war that ran off and on from 1350 to 1500, in which the whole north was divided into factions, based on bonds of family, finances or fickleness. It was a bloody mess.

Ymke shares more of my family's history than we'd originally planned. My grandmother died when my mom was 14, and very soon she was taken out of school, and sent to work as a maid at a local farm. It was the late '50s, during the last years of a sort of indentured servitude system; just a decade earlier, girls as young as 12 would be sent to work and live at farms for small wages, with just Sunday afternoons off. She wasn't as badly off as those girls had been, and she did go home every day, though there she also had to do the housekeeping and cook for my grandfather.

What Ymke also got from my mother is her bad leg. My mom was born with hip dysplasia, but rather than have her treated (my brother spent his baby years in leg braces) my grandfather thought she'd grow out of it. Of course, she didn't, and eventually she had her first hip replacement in her mid-thirties. I've only known her as walking badly, or worse.

How much does the imaginary world you have created together bear the stamp of your lived experiences?

Our world has grown and sprawled with the ideas we've chosen to explore, from unusual people coming together in a big city, to rural loneliness and isolation. It's very obviously a world where people have learned to live on the margins. Religion is sometimes a benign influence interpersonally, but as part of the larger social structure, it's oppressive, and I grew up in a place with a decades-long armed conflict in which religion is a huge factor.

We've both experienced bullying in our lives, whether that's from individuals at school, or a government that makes propaganda against immigrants and disabled people. Ymke and Kaila take a stand against men who exploit women, because misogyny looms large in our world. The Brotherhood of the Wheel is every fundamentalist, bigoted, reactionary religious and political force that has shaped our lives. At different stages in the stories, we see it as a small localised phenomenon, and as a growing threat, and it's also very clear that such things must be opposed.

Rogues in the House **podcast called** ***The Red Man and Others*** **'New Wave Sword and Sorcery'. Is that true, and what is 'New Wave Sword and Sorcery'?**

Angeline: I think the New Wave has already been around for some time. Actually, the New Wave was the generation of Sword and Sorcery writers who first reacted against your standard barbarians like Conan, Thongor and Brak; writers like Michael Moorcock, Charles R. Saunders and Tanith Lee come to mind. One thing that has worried us lately is the ease with which parts of the canon can slip out of readers' hands. When Sword and Soul trailblazer Charles R. Saunders died earlier this year, it took months for the news to spread through fandom. Through his hero Imaro, his other fiction and his non-fiction writing, Saunders expanded the tradition. Yet much of his short fiction remains uncollected, and fans are currently fundraising in order that he might have a headstone. Maintaining the canon is an ongoing work. There are stirrings of hope - Tanith Lee's work is finally becoming more available in ebook form, and we hope that will extend to books like *Kill the Dead*, in whose tradition our work rests. That book and others like it have had a huge influence on how we approach character, world building and atmosphere. So, we're not actually *that* bleeding edge, but since we still have the stubborn contingent of stalwarts and throwbacks, New Wave is a standard we will happily bear onwards.

We don't live in a world that is just white, heterosexual and able-bodied. Kaila and Ymke come from very different cultural backgrounds, with Ymke a white farmer's daughter and Kaila from a Middle East analogue, having hauled herself over a mountain range and fought herself to where and when we meet her. Their love reflects the frustrations we've heard from so many friends about how LGBTQ characters get relegated to the gay but single best friend trope. But we're drawing on very old influences, too: ever since Robert E. Howard, the woman who rises up against male oppression has been an intrinsic part of the genre. We've just pushed it, and brought them to the foreground.

You both have a substantial background in journalism. You have interviewed authors like Neil Jordan, James Ellroy and Anne Rice, and your piece for *Fortean Times* about writer Robert E. Howard received a REH Foundation Award nomination. Tell us more about your work and how important it is to you both.

The main thing we've learned from interviewing people is that there's always a story that hasn't been told. Before meeting or sending questions to authors like the ones you've mentioned, we would usually over-prepare, reading through their recent and past interviews to see what fresh spin we could put on the questions. We would skip the questions that had been asked a thousand times already, and often that would be rewarded.

There's a bit of magic that happens when you get a conversation going and people give you more than you asked for, and we were always very touched by the generosity of subjects who were sometimes talking about intensely personal matters. James Ellroy, for example, we found to be very friendly and not at all the character he plays on stage, and Neil Jordan intuited better than we what deeper themes could be explored in our interview with him.

I think that extends to writing fiction - there's always more to people, and as an author you can feel like you're discovering, un-covering people as much as inventing them, because your own life ex-perience and your intuition start to work, especially when you've got to know characters well. There's an interplay of familiarity and sur-prise, when you realise something about them that you didn't expect.

What about the humour in the book, which is mentioned by several reviewers?

We write about some serious, painful and traumatic things, but they're happening to people, and the gap between perception and reality, whether it's someone's reputation or how they see themselves, is often a rich vein of comedy. We find ourselves pushing situations further and further, until they become absurd, and then we need to backpedal again, so as not to end up with shaggy dog stories and caricatures.

There's a wonderful *Calvin and Hobbes* strip where Bill Watterson has the characters discussing how strange it is that we have a physiological reaction to absurdity, and one of them says that since so much of life is absurd, without laughter, we would have no way of responding to it. I think it's fair to say that our life experiences have given us a great appreciation of the absurd, as well as the morbidly funny.

We've always wanted to write like Robert E. Howard, but we end up closer to Fritz Leiber. Humour comes to us naturally but unbidden, and we decided to see it as a feature, not a bug. The classic horror films are enjoyed best when you recognise the humour in them too. It's an old recipe, the sandwich formula that was used in Grand Guignol, to switch humour and horror. You'll see this really clearly in James Whale's *Bride of Frankenstein*, which you can only properly enjoy when you recognise it as an exercise in camp and irony.

Angeline, you say of Ymke, the protagonist of *The Red Man* and *The Return of the Uncomplaining Child*: 'Ymke's rebellions, like mine, have often been subtle ones: staying alive in a world that oppresses disabled people is also a form of resistance. But sometimes we're both surprised by what we're capable of doing when we really have to - and with the right person by our side.' How important are Ymke's rebellions in the book?

Angeline: Over the course of *The Red Man*, Ymke learns to defy her father, and she does it repeatedly. They've been a team in this strange, lonely life, and until the Red Man comes into their lives she's trusted her father's view of the world completely: that it's a threatening place, and the only logical, safe response to that is hiding.

When she goes out into the world, she starts by trying to play by its rules, and she quickly realises that it's absurd (that word again!) trying to make a living in a way that exploits her labour at every turn - forced to grind away doing poorly paid work for greedy bosses in order to gain a scribe's certification, she forges the thing herself. Sometimes an unfair system deserves to be undermined, and that finds its fullest expression when she, Kaila and Sebastien give the Brotherhood of the Wheel what they think they want: the Return of the Uncomplaining Child.

Remco, you talk of discovering the Conan series by Robert E. Howard as a teenager. How have your feelings about the books developed over time?

Remco: I read the first Conan stories when I was 15, and for me they literally were escapism. I was having a rough time at school, and this was a world for me to flee into. These weren't even the best of Conan stories; the collection was a translation of *Conan the Wanderer*, a mix of pastiche and rewritten non-Conan tales. It stuck with me though: first through the Dutch version of the Marvel comics with Windsor-Smith, and Buscema as artist; more paperbacks, and as I moved out to study, the *Savage Sword of Conan* magazines.

I also found a stack of fanzines from the '70s and got a bit more fundamentalist: Howard – good; DeCamp and Carter – bad! I've mellowed since, and am perfectly happy for people to enjoy their DeCamp and Carter. I do like DeCamp's own books, but he's not a great fit for Conan, while Lin Carter is a great editor. As for Howard – I've read his Conan stories again in my late 20s and, without interference, were better than I remembered them to be. Since then I've dipped into the stories here and there, and knowing more about Howard himself, I can see how his own life and personality are present in the best of them.

Tell us more about *The Return of the Uncomplaining Child...*

That story came about when on holiday in Kent. We bought a book on Joan of Arc, and there was a chapter on the Joan of Arc imposters, including Claude des Armoises who convinced many, including Joan's brothers. We got intrigued by the idea of historical usurpers and imposters, like the Anastasia claimants, and the mechanics of how they managed to get away with their deceit, and why people who knew the originals believed in them.

We'd already introduced the idea of the Uncomplaining Child in *Road to Starohrad*, and we got talking about the idea of what would happen if the dead saint appeared to come back to life: how would people react to him; what would it reveal about their better (or worse) natures? It was an obvious job for Sebastien, which meant Kaila would also get involved, and it hit us that Ymke really needed to meet those two. Together, they would cook up a scam, the women would fall in love, and we would make satirical hay with the whole thing.

There's a lot of personal frustrations in Ymke's experiences as a scribe, but the larger problem of a bullying cult throwing their weight about comes from the fact that we both grew up in societies that have their share of religious intolerance. Places where there are shibboleths to identify which tradition of Christianity someone grew up in, or where hanging laundry on a Sunday means your neighbour's child will throw mud at it to punish you for your Sabbath labour. In both places, religious hatred has often kindled into violence.

At the same time, faith is a tremendous source of strength to people in both communities. Sebastien's extended performance as the Uncomplaining Child has unexpected effects on him and his friends, as well as the wider community. What happens when you give people something to believe in, and it's fake, but the goodwill that grows up around it is real? Do you puncture the illusion? Is the good you've done real, or is it compromised by the deception?

We also had fun with the city of Otasring here; it's city of tall buildings and small windows, perched on top of a giant rock, in a forest with massive trees. This city is an amalgam of Brunhild's rock-perched fortress and the city of Worms as they appear in Fritz Lang's *Nibelungen* films. You've also got Kaila and Ymke bonding over the people's dramatic style of clothing, all long gowns and large geometric patterns, and they suspect that the forest with the giant trees from which the Otasringar come has engraved itself on their psyche. We like to tell stories within our stories, and create bits of mythology and legend.

What books are you reading at the moment and have you got any favourites?

Angeline: I'm reading *Disability Visibility*, edited by Alice Wong, which collects personal stories of disability, resistance and resilience, as well as *The Interior Life* by Katherine Blake, a fantasy novel in which we learn that you underestimate the wives and housekeepers of the world at your peril.

Remco: I've finished a Gardner Fox *Kothar* paperback recently, and enjoyed it quite a bit: it knew what it wanted to be, and did it well. At least its female anti-hero had agency. Now I'm in Mary Renault's first *Theseus* novel, *The King Must Die*. We've got our own Minotaur tale to tell one day, and Renault set the bar for historical fiction pretty high, even 60 years ago. Hers is not a retelling of Theseus' story, but a telling of the story how it could have been before it became myth. I love this texturing with truth, story and myth, and the truth in myth. That's why you'll often find snippets, whether true or not, of a deeper history in our stories and characters. Mary Renault changed the Theseus from legend into a wiry teenager who gradually finds out about his past while he confronts, and shapes, his history. What he reveals about himself to others, and what he chooses to believe about himself, are not objectively true. We all create our own personal myth, out of necessity or expediency, and we're definitely allowing our characters to do the same.

Please tell your readers something about your blog, *Turnip Lanterns*, and your interest in folklore.

Angeline: The blog is a collection of passions of ours, many of which inform the world of *The Red Man and Others*: we explore our interests in folklore and history, and we dig deep into things we love and that have been a big influence on our work, from comics to films to books. From a marketing perspective, it's not the best way to run a blog: the advice is to stick to a subject and an easily recognised theme, but we like to cast our net wider. We're of a generation whose formative entertainment, made in the '70s and '80s, was very much imbued with the historical, folkloric and supernatural, and *The Red Man* in particular fits into that tradition, which is now being explored and reflected on more and more in pop culture and through commentary online, like *The Haunted Generation* or *Folk Horror Revival*. By a fluke, we both grew up very influenced by living history museums: my father was Dialect Archivist at the Ulster Folk and Transport Museum, and Remco worked at Verhildersum Museum in Leens in his late teens, so the past is very much alive for us, but also subject to interrogation and reflection.

The format gives us the freedom to explore and bring together topics like genre fiction and issues of identity. Recently we highlighted the female readership of *Weird Tales* throughout its history. We spoke out about the resistance in some parts of Sword and Sorcery to the diverse readership (and authorship!) we enjoy today, and we've written about the significance of speculative fiction to autistic fans.

What are you planning next?

Angeline: We've got plenty more stories and a novella for the Red Man world, at varying stages of completion. They're ambitious, and we hope unexpected - we're trying to give readers more of what they've told us they love about these characters and their world, while stretching the boundaries. We wanted to meet the characters at very different points in their lifetimes and see how they've influenced each other - and changed their world.

We have other projects on the back burner, too - there's a historical novel set in that northern Groningen village of Ulrum in the mid-19th century. It will be about a writer who lived there who was also a folklorist, colonial administrator and, as a result, an abolitionist. His legacy has largely fallen by the wayside, partly because he was a fierce critic of a local preacher who schismed off the Dutch Reformed Church and still has a large flock in the village, and partly because he's primarily seen as 'a failed farmer.' We think it's time his story was told.

Lastly, we have another fantasy project coalescing in the background: it features vampires, steampunk, and a pair of lovers who are not what they seem...

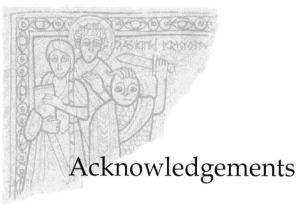

Acknowledgements

Writing is not such an isolated endeavour as it may seem. We know this from writing as a couple, and also because *The Red Man and Others* would not have come into being, or found its readership, without the support, cheerleading and signal boosting from various friends, colleagues and critics.

Already in 2015, Regina Lizik convinced us that what was to become *Road to Starohrad* had legs, and that people would want to get to know our characters better. She also restored our sense of perspective at a crucial point and convinced us that talk of 'breaking of wheels' in *Game of Thrones* was not as big a deal as we thought, and that besides Robert Jordan was there first.

Beau Watkins was another early supporter of our writing, a catcher of unfortunate typos, and a reassuring sounding board as we grappled with the business end of fiction.

Ricardo Pinto convinced us that self-publishing was a viable option, and an attractive one. We'd be lost without his support, encouragement and example, from the writing all the way through to the current paper edition. His reworked *Stone Dance of the Chameleon* septet gave us something to aspire to in all its attention to detail, and his meticulousness saved us from many errors and oddities in our own manuscript. Without Ricardo, this book would not be what it is – or indeed, there might not be a book at all.

Coreo Jones understood and believed in this book from the start, and helped us make the agricultural and equine aspects believable. Their feedback on *The Return of the Uncomplaining Child* was brilliantly thorough and practical, and strengthened the story enormously, while their caps-locked enthusiasm spurred us on.

We've also been delighted to have the support of Logan Whitney at *Rogues in the House*, and Ngo Vinh-Hoi at *Appendix N Book Club*. We know we're doing something a bit different where Sword & Sorcery is concerned, but podcasts like these prove that the genre is open to wider horizons and a more diverse readership we always hoped were out there. Likewise, Jessica Rydill and Cora Buhlert of Speculative Fiction Showcase gave us a precious opportunity to talk about the book in depth, and kindly allowed us to reproduce that interview here.

And after all that, many of you showed up for the book on social media. It feels unkind to pick names, but we would be remiss not to acknowledge the particular support of Victoria Audley, Rae Knowler and Elizabeth Anne Grummitt, to say nothing of the patience our friends displayed as we learned how to be first-time publishers on an eye-wateringly ambitious timescale.

And on that note, we've been fortunate to discover the writing community Otherworlds NI, who continue to support, inspire and teach us, and to grow our to-read piles to infinity. We're also indebted to our wider online community, which has been our social lifeline through the isolation of both chronic illness and the pandemic.

It also feels important to recognise here that the book came into being during an unbelievably difficult and frightening period of our lives. I don't think we would have felt able to approach this project without the support of friends who got us through everything from interminable hospital stays to illness at WorldCon, and the past year, which saw us self-isolating. If you were there with us, you know who you are.

Angeline & Remco
March 2, 2021

Printed in Great Britain
by Amazon